FLY ME HOME

Polly used to be a primary-school teacher in London and while she was teaching there she used to get up very early in the morning to write stories. The first of those stories became a book called *Boy in the Tower*.

She's still writing stories and, though these days she doesn't teach, she does often visit schools . . . only now they're all over the country.

She lives in Bristol with her husband, Dan, who designs the covers of her books.

Books by Polly Ho-Yen

BOY IN THE TOWER
WHERE MONSTERS LIE
FLY ME HOME

FLY ME HOME

POLLY HO-YEN

CORGI BOOKS

CORGI BOOKS

UK | USA | Canada | Ireland | Australia
India | New Zealand | South Africa

Corgi Books is part of the Penguin Random House group of companies
whose addresses can be found at global.penguinrandomhouse.com.

www.penguin.co.uk
www.puffin.co.uk
www.ladybird.co.uk

First published 2017

001

Typeset in 11.5/15.5 pt ITC New Baskerville Std
by Jouve (UK), Milton Keynes
Printed in Great Britain by Clays Ltd, St Ives plc

A CIP catalogue record for this book is available from the British Library

ISBN: 978–0–552–57623–9

All correspondence to:
Corgi Books
Penguin Random House Children's
80 Strand, London WC2R 0RL

MIX
Paper from
responsible sources
FSC® C018179

Penguin Random House is committed to a
sustainable future for our business, our readers
and our planet. This book is made from Forest
Stewardship Council® certified paper.

This book is dedicated to the very dear Doyle-Finch family
(both two-footed and four-footed members alike)

Prologue

'Can't you come with us? Can't we go together?'

I grasped the smallest piece of Dad's shirt tightly in my hand, but I felt him unpick my fingers one by one until he was holding my hand in his.

'I can't, my sweet pea,' he said softly. He looked like he wanted to say something more, but he stayed quiet.

'I don't want to go,' I said. 'Not without you.'

There was a well opening up inside me. I could feel it lengthening, deepening, widening, with every breath I took.

'You must go,' Dad said. 'You've got to stay safe . . . I mean . . . what I mean is, you're going to have a great adventure. You and your mum and Tiber – you're going to find us a new home. You can get everything ready for when I get there. Find the best places to go! The best things to eat!'

He was smiling now, and he squeezed my sides in a way he knew would tickle, make me wriggle and jump.

I darted away so that he couldn't reach me, and as I moved I heard him laugh.

It started small, in his belly, and then grew and grew until it seemed to fill the whole room. It made me imagine the dome of his tummy lighting up, all aglow. I wished I could capture that sound, bottle it, fold it into the clothes in our suitcase, bury it deep in my pocket.

I couldn't leave it behind.

'Leelu!' Mum was shouting for me to go through the barrier now. As I turned to look for her, Dad let go of my hand, and when I looked back, he was striding away. Out of reach.

Mum swept me up in a chaos of bags and coats and tickets, and walked me through the barrier and away.

And Dad . . . Well, Dad we left behind.

We got on the plane, and when it took off I felt a vague sort of sickness rolling around inside me like a marble. I told myself it was from being in the cabin, but I knew it was really because we had left Dad behind. I wondered if he was still standing in the airport. Maybe he thought we might run back to him . . .

Mum said I should try to sleep but I couldn't. Then she said I should close my eyes anyway and keep them closed, and that was when I dreamed of him.

I dreamed of Dad. Not standing in the airport, not clasping my hand or striding away, but flying. I dreamed of him flying.

I could see him flying next to us – right by the plane, by the solid white angles of its wing. I could see him through the small rounded square of the window.

He didn't have wings or anything like that; he just had his arms down by his sides, but he was definitely flying. I slept on, content in the fiction that we hadn't left him behind; he was coming with us after all.

But it was just a dream, of course. When I woke up, Mum was asking me if I wanted some orange juice, and there was nothing to see outside apart from a heavy layer of grey cloud that became darker and darker as I looked at it.

Because people can't really fly.

Dreams don't come true.

1

The first thing I noticed was the cold.

It crept around my bare legs.

My shoulders started to shake, then shudder, as though I was unfurling a pair of wings that, until then, I hadn't known I possessed.

'This is it,' Mum said. A tight smile. It did not quite stretch across her face.

We took our first steps out of the aeroplane, Mum, Tiber and me, doddering, unsure of where to step, unsure of how our bodies moved, like we were babies taking our first few steps on brand-new, chubby legs.

I looked back across the tarmac runway before I turned into the airport – a building that was full of fluorescent lights and noise and signs with arrows pointing this way and that.

Lights were studded across the runway in pathways and lines. Little pinpricks in the darkness.

It looked hard.
Cold.
Grey.
Our new home.

2

I found the first surprise on our first day here.

It was tucked into a little sliver of space outside our new house, between the bin and the metal lamppost beside it. There, crammed in at an angle so it wouldn't fall: a walnut.

It sounds strange, I suppose, to notice something so small, so insignificant. Perhaps it was because of the way it had been placed there. Wedged in securely, waiting for me.

Mum always tuts when she sees the bin and the rubbish just outside our front door. That day, some old wooden drawers had been left next to the bin. Their sides were coming apart and the rain had swelled the wood so they were sodden, ruined. And a torn bag of rubbish had spilled its innards onto the street: dried-out grey chicken bones and the greasy red-and-yellow boxes that had once housed them.

Every day, when we opened our thin blue front door, we found another lot of things left there. Old fridges, the plugs snipped off so that the wires stuck out wonkily. Broken toys missing wheels or eyes.

But mostly it was food.

It rotted and stank, filling the air with a putrid, sour smell that coated your skin, lingered in your hair.

Mum always shut the door securely each time we got back to the house, pressing her weight against it to close the latch properly, as though she could stop the smell from coming in. When that didn't work, she slammed the door hard; the force made the walls shudder.

Of course, smells won't let a door stand in their way. They creep through cracks, whisper through gaps, find their way through the smallest of spaces. Our house always smelled of old rubbish, no matter how much we cleaned it or how many cans of air freshener Mum emptied into the stale rooms.

After a while I got used to it, although I'm not sure that Mum ever did.

I got used to her tutting whenever she saw the rubbish too. It was as sure as the bleep that Tiber's watch made on every hour.

Mum taught herself to swing her gaze away from the bin and whatever had been dumped there that day, but I always found myself drawn to it.

It was because of the old walnut I found there on our first day here.

It had a hard shell that was smooth and mottled at the same time. The nut rattled when I shook it.

Sometimes I imagined that if I broke it open, I wouldn't find a nut at all but some kind of magical jewel. A ruby like a luminous berry; a diamond that looked like ice.

But I never cracked it open.

I'd pulled it from its place suspended between the ground, the bin and the lamppost and held it tightly in my hand so Mum wouldn't see it and tell me to drop it.

It became warm there, clasped in my palm, and when I examined it later, it seemed to give off its own heat. As though it was alive.

I held it carefully, as I would something treasured or delicate: the photograph of Mum, Dad, Tiber and me set in heavy glass and edged in silver; my grandmother's tiny jug, the porcelain worn thin by use.

But I didn't know, couldn't have dreamed how precious that old walnut truly was.

3

I hid the walnut under a loose floorboard I'd found by my bed.

It had only become my bed after Tiber and I fought over it.

Tiber and I fought over lots of things. Small, petty things mostly. Things that neither of us cared about really. It came to us as naturally as breathing. We'd tussle back and forth, pushing and pulling, and then, somewhere along the line, we'd drop it. Because, as I said, our fights didn't usually matter that much to us. The point was more about disagreeing with each other.

Sometimes, though, they did. And on those occasions Tiber would know. He'd sniff it out without me having said a word. He wouldn't let it drop. Tiber was five years older than me. Sometimes he seemed much older, but there were other times, especially when we fought, when there seemed to be no age difference at all. As if any wisdom he had gained in those years when I was not yet in the world vanished with the opportunity to rile, provoke and tease.

'He only wants it because I do,' I cried out. 'It's bad enough that we have to share a room here . . .'

Tiber made a whining copy of my voice.

'Shut up, Tiber!'

'Hey!' Mum said to me sharply. A warning.

I tried to ignore my grinning brother making faces at me when Mum's back was turned. He pulled his mouth wide with two fingers so it looked rectangular, like a letter box.

'Please, Mum,' I said.

She sighed and then reached into her purse for a penny. 'Heads or tails?'

I sighed too. This was something Dad did whenever we got into an argument over something and couldn't agree. I'd learned not to question it, however annoying I thought Tiber was being. Dad said it was the only fair way of deciding sometimes.

'Tails,' I said quietly.

'All right then. Tails, Leelu gets the bed by the window. Heads, Tiber does.'

Mum looked round at Tiber, who had managed to stop pulling faces just in time. He nodded his head demurely in agreement.

She threw the coin high into the air; it sailed upwards, almost to the ceiling, somersaulting as it did so.

Tails, tails, tails, I thought. With every bit of me.

Sometimes I wondered whether, if you wanted something badly enough, you could make it happen. Just by the power of thought.

Of course, it didn't always work. Before leaving our home I'd thought hard about Dad coming with us. It was something to do with his work: it meant that he couldn't come at the same time but would follow us later.

I'd concentrated with every bit of me on the thought that he would come too, but it didn't matter how much I imagined us all staying together, we had still left without him.

One of the reasons I wanted the bed by the window was to do with Dad.

It had been hard to leave him. There had been what felt like hours and hours of waiting at the airport. Tiber and I had gone off for little walks because we'd got bored of sitting in one place. Later, I wished I had never left Dad's side. When the time came to say goodbye, there suddenly weren't enough seconds left.

I felt his arms release me before I did him, and I only let go when he said, 'We'll always have the moon, Leelu. We'll have the moon.'

'What you mean?' I said, sniffing through the words.

'Wherever I am, I'll look for it. At night-time, when the day is done. I'll sit on our old, rickety chair in the porch. I'll be listening to the grass-hoppers. I'll look up at that moon and know that you are there, looking too. All the way off in London, I'll know that you are looking at it. Look at it now – it's a full moon tonight. Can you see it?'

I'd let go of Dad to turn towards the sky. The moon sat round and white, solemn-looking, in the black sky.

'Can you see that crater right at the top? That's where I'll look for you. Can you do that for me? Look for our crater in the moon?'

I blinked the tears from my eyes so that I could look at it properly. 'Which crater?'

'That one, at the top on the right. The one that sits by itself. Can you see it?'

'Yes,' I said, staring at the crater; it was so far away it looked like only a circle.

'That crater will be our place,' Dad said. 'Just you and me. No one else will know.' He kissed the top of my head. It made a light, plucking sound. Then he placed his palms firmly on my shoulders and squeezed. It was meant to be comforting but it made me feel trapped. As though the pressure of his hands would quieten me, stop me from rising up, reacting.

'But how will I know when to look at it?' I blurted out. Prickles rose up my back. I felt as though I was growing spikes, spiny and sharp to the touch. 'How will I know when you'll be looking at it?'

'OK,' Dad said. 'Let's think. You'll be one hour behind in the UK, so what if I look out at ten o'clock my time? That'll be your bedtime – nine o'clock. Look out then, at nine. At bedtime. OK?'

I didn't have time to answer him. There was some sort of muffled announcement about our flight, and Mum said, 'We have to go,' in a dead, flat voice that made me look away. Suddenly, after all the waiting, it was a rush. We grabbed our bags and scrambled towards the part of the airport where Dad could no longer follow.

'Goodbye! Goodbye, my sweet peas,' I heard him shout. 'I'll see you soon. I love you.' He said 'you' in a way that lasted, like he was singing the last note of a song. I remember thinking, *How could he possibly sound so happy, so full of joy, at the sight of us leaving?*

I looked at him over my shoulder. The white of his teeth was framed by a grin. One of his hands rested on the slight dome of his belly and the other was outstretched, fingers splayed in a jubilant wave.

It was only his eyes that gave him away. They were wide with worry, strained with sadness, desperate to reach us.

'Dad!' I called out, but I was being carried away by the tide of people. I fought against them, even though Tiber said, 'Don't look back.' At first I thought he was being mean, but then he added in a low voice, 'It's easier if you don't look back.'

But I didn't want it easy. I struggled to get back to Dad, and when I reached him, breathless and desperate, my hand grabbed the first bit of him that I touched. The corner of his old shirt. I remember thinking that I would never let it go. I would just never loosen my grip.

Can't you come with us? Can't we go together?

I'd asked those questions countless times, but no matter how many times I asked them or Mum and Dad answered them, I never felt that I fully understood why we were leaving. Or why it was that Dad wasn't coming with us.

What with the flight and finding somewhere to live, I hadn't managed to look out at the moon at the right time since we'd arrived.

Part of me thought it was a silly thing to do. I didn't think it would make me feel closer to Dad. Not really. But despite these thoughts, I still wanted that bed next to the window. I had to try and look for Dad's crater.

I had to see if it would work. Whether just looking at that grey patch on the moon might make the pain I felt at having to leave him just a little more bearable.

4

There was another reason why I wanted the bed by the window.

It was to do with the loose floorboard I had found.

I discovered it when our greasy-looking landlord, Mr Abenezzi, was showing us around the house. It had been night-time already. We'd all felt exhausted in that way that makes everything around you feel disconnected, unreal, just out of reach. In the harsh light of the bare bulbs that hung from each off-white ceiling, each room looked as unwelcoming as the next. But there was no question that we were not going to move in that night, whatever the house was like. We had all our bags with us, piled up in the hallway.

I missed our old house, which was so familiar to me that I could walk around it with my eyes closed. If all the lights went out, which sometimes happened when we had a power cut, I could navigate my way through the rooms easily, without a stumble; I knew them so well. But here, even in the glare of the bare bulbs, I tripped on sharp edges of furniture, I knocked my knees on the narrow doorways and bruised my elbow on the banister, which stuck out awkwardly.

Our old kitchen was big enough for a table in the middle, where we always sat for our meals. 'No excuses!' Dad would say if Tiber tried to sneak his plate away to eat in another room. 'This table is where we talk and eat and share!' When he said this, he would throw his hands up in the air expansively and the table would rock. One of the legs would bang against the floor, as though it was joining in with the conversation.

Dad wouldn't like this new place, where the kitchen and the living room were all in one room. Everything was squashed together, so the only place you could sit was on the long sofa that sagged in the middle.

I strained my eyes, looking for some colour, some character in those blank boxy rooms, but there was none; only thin walls; beige, stained spaces.

While Mum was talking to Mr Abenezzi about money, and Tiber had gone out to the small, dank patch of concrete that Mr Abenezzi had called 'great outside space', I sneaked away. Upstairs, I looked round the little room that would become mine and Tiber's. Neither of us wanted to share a room, but as we'd walked between the two bedrooms upstairs and realized that one was for Mum and the other for us, Mum had simply shrugged her shoulders and said, 'We'll have to make do.'

We whined and groaned, but nothing we said made another bedroom magically appear.

The room we'd share was a very small rectangle, full of flimsy fake-wood furniture. When I sat on the bed by the window, the mattress wheezed and creaked as though it was complaining. The headboard bumped against the wall in an alarming rattle.

That was when I saw it.

Just next to the bed there was a tear in the thin, stained carpet, which pulled back easily to show the dusty floorboards underneath. With a bit of wiggling, one of the small, crooked boards came loose to reveal a little hiding place under the floor.

It was dark in there, and when I first put my hand into the black hole, I thought I felt something furry and pulled it back in shock. But when I looked more closely, I saw that it was only a thick layer of grey dust that stuck together when I lifted it out. It disintegrated in my fingers and scattered over the carpet.

The space under the floorboard was not much bigger than a shoebox, but it was more than enough for me to hide a few things, out of Tiber's reach, away from Mum's eyes. It would be a little place of my own, here, in a home where we did not belong.

As I studied it, I heard voices approaching up the stairs. I quickly put back the floorboard and covered it all up with the carpet, just as I had found it. When Mum appeared, I was sitting on the bed, looking out of the window.

'You like it here, Leelu?' she asked.

'It's OK,' I said slowly. It was just that: OK. Not terrible. Not wonderful. And definitely not home.

'I think we're going to have to take it,' Mum said, staring at the carpet. 'I know it's not ideal with you two sharing a room, but it's all we can afford.' She leaned against the chest of drawers, and as she did so, it made a shifting, buckling sound. She stood up again quickly, unsettled.

'If we do live here . . . can I have this bed?' I asked.

'I don't see why not,' Mum said.

'No, that's *my* bed,' Tiber said, appearing at the door, smiling.

And's that how it all started, with Mum doing the coin toss.

The coin was spinning, spinning in the air as though suspended there, and then it began to fall.

Suddenly I knew that the coin would land and it would be heads. Tiber would win.

He would stroll over to the bed and jump onto it in a single movement, like a cat, except that his weight would make the bed frame creak and shudder.

I had to do something. I looked around for a distraction; in desperation, I even delved into my pockets.

That was when I felt the walnut.

The walnut I had found between the bin and the lamppost.

It felt reassuringly hard, and as I clasped it, I thought I felt it twitch, although I knew that was impossible.

It was just the tiniest little shift, and then it was over.

Tails, tails, tails, I thought. And then: *Please let me have the bed so that I can look at the moon and be closer to Dad. I miss him so much.*

The walnut gave another twitch, more definite this time.

As I felt its vibration, I swiftly released it.

The coin landed on Mum's open hand.

She deftly smacked her palm over it so we couldn't see which way up it was. Tiber leaned in closer.

Mum drew her hand away.

I didn't look.

I knew it was tails.

I knew that the bed was mine.

'Tails. Leelu gets the bed,' Mum said.

'Best of three?' Tiber asked.

'Nice try,' she said, walking away.

I lay down on the bed, my bed, and Tiber stalked off, muttering something about fairness or unfairness.

I took the walnut out of my pocket and held it carefully in my hand.

It lay quite still. It didn't move again.

It looked just like an ordinary walnut.

5

A few days after I found the walnut I saw something else lodged in exactly the same place, just between the bin and the lamppost.

At first I thought it was another walnut. It looked roughly the same size and shape, but as I approached, I saw that it wasn't honey-coloured. It was darker. It collected more shadows.

Its wooden, ridged body looked a little like the armour worn by the characters in Tiber's old comics. Only brown of course. Not colourful and loud.

I took it, as I had the walnut, looking around to see where it might have come from.

It could have fallen from a tree, but the ones that grew on our street, tall and sheltering, with yellow and brown bark that looked like it was falling off, didn't grow anything like this.

Or walnuts, for that matter.

Someone had placed it there very carefully. They had wedged it into the space between the bin and the lamppost so that it wouldn't fall.

Did they want it to be found? Had they known what the walnut could do?

At that moment Tiber came bursting out of the house behind me so I hid it deep in my pocket. I ran my fingers over its ridges, which felt like miniature mountains and valleys.

'Wotcha doing?' Tiber looked at me with his head slightly cocked to one side.

'Nothing,' I replied, letting go of whatever it was. I tucked a strand of hair behind my ear unnecessarily, nervously, to give my hand something to do.

'Looks like you're up to something,' Tiber said. I wondered, not for the first time, how, even when I was doing everything I could to keep a secret from him, he could know me so well.

'Nope.' I kept my face blank.

I didn't want to share it with him in case he lobbed it in the air and it flew away from me for ever. Tiber's very fond of throwing things, especially if they don't belong to him.

Just then we heard loud music start up in the house next to us. It was inhabited by people we called the Noisy Neighbours; there were so many of them living there – I couldn't understand how they all managed to fit in.

'Right on time,' Tiber said as the bass started to throb in the air. We hadn't met our neighbours properly, but we had come to know them from looking out of the window and hearing them. The Noisy Neighbours were on one side; on the other lived a very old man. We never heard any noise coming from his house, but we knew he had a huge, hairy grey dog, as big as a wolf, which looked like it might bite you if it got the chance. I refused to go out when I saw the old man shuffling along the street with his dog.

There were voices coming from the Noisy Neighbours' house, and what sounded like a cat screeching in pain. Suddenly their front door flew open and a group of boys spilled out, chasing a football between them. They ran across the pavement and into the road.

They all looked alike, their skin golden brown, their hair tousled and dark. They moved together, like a pack: a single creature with multiple skinny legs and arms.

Just then a car came speeding round the corner towards them. I heard Tiber suck his teeth as it careened down the road, tyres screeching, engine roaring.

All but one of the boys dashed back onto the pavement as it charged towards them. All but the smallest, who chased after the football, which had rolled out into the middle of the road.

'Hey! Betsy!' one of the boys shouted out. 'Leave it! Get out of the road!'

The smallest boy, I realized, was not a boy at all.

She leaned back, glanced towards the pavement, a laughing look on her face, and then, about as fast as I had seen anyone move, sprinted towards the ball, which had dribbled its way into the path of the car.

She caught up with it before the car met her. Then, in what looked like one movement, neatly hooked her foot around the ball, stopping it in its tracks, and kicked it forcefully back towards us.

The car rushed past in a blur, obliterating the girl from view.

'Betsy!' another of the boys shouted, his voice panicked.

'What's the problem?' she said, stepping out from the other side of the road, arms and eyebrows raised quizzically.

The boys grumbled something in a language I did not understand.

'Come on, let's play,' said Betsy.

There was more grumbling, but the ball was dropped on the ground again and the boys chased it down, moving as one, each face indistinguishable from the others.

We heard their shouts long after they had disappeared round the corner. I was sure I heard more dismayed cries of 'Betsy!' and wondered what dangerous thing that small, scruffy-haired girl was up to now. She was so utterly fearless, I couldn't help but be fascinated by her.

Then Mum suddenly appeared in the doorway.

Her nose wrinkled at the sight of the new lot of rubbish abandoned by the bin and she looked determinedly away from it. She hurried us down the street, simultaneously taking my hand and removing from Tiber's an old can that he had picked up off the pavement and was about to chuck across the road.

'Let's get to know this place,' she said.

We walked down one of the roads and Mum muttered something like, 'Yes, this is the right way,' but to me, each street looked identical. Dark and grey, with nothing to distinguish one from another. The blocks of flats that surrounded us looked the same from every angle; large brown boxy buildings.

Our feet slapped down hard on the tarmac pavement, and for some reason the sound of our footsteps made me feel very tired.

'Nearly there,' trilled Mum when we heard cars ahead of us.

We walked down a road that heaved and groaned with cars in search of something to eat, some place warm to sit.

6

We stopped at the first place we came to. It was a
fried-chicken shop.

Tiber bolted his portion, and then started
begging us to give him some of ours.

'You've had enough,' Mum said, but he
continued to plead and beg until I tossed him one
of my chicken legs just to keep him quiet.

'Thanks, Lulu,' he said. 'You're my favourite
sister.'

'I'm your only sister,' I said back.

The chicken was greasy and left slippery patches
of oil on our fingers. After just one piece I no longer
felt hungry and let Tiber have the rest – and my
chips too. He scoffed them down; it was hard to hear
the words 'thank you' through all the chewing.

Mum didn't eat much either, and elbowed her
paper plate towards Tiber; delighted, he worked
his way through most of her dinner as well.

'Not hungry, Mum?' I asked her.

'Not too much,' she said, smiling at me. It was a quick, small smile, peeking out like the sun does here when it appears from behind one cloud, only to disappear behind another.

Mum looked around the restaurant. It was very bright, lit by long fluorescent tubes. One of them flickered every now and again; each time it did, Mum shivered and closed her eyes.

'Let's go . . .' she said when Tiber had sucked clean the last of the chicken bones, but she didn't finish the sentence. In the end she said, 'Let's go . . . back.'

She didn't want to call the house we lived in now our home, and I understood why. Everything was so different here.

I felt as though I hadn't seen colour, not properly, since we arrived. I wondered if colour like we had at home would be able to survive in these grey concrete streets. Everything was brighter there. The sunshine, the colour of the grass. The paint on the houses, the clothes. The gleam in everyone's eyes. In London there seemed to be only tones of grey, as though everything was awash with it. From the roads to the trees to the faces of the people we passed.

Maybe if we saw colour now, it would blind us. It would be too bright; our eyes weren't accustomed to it any more.

Perhaps we had got too used to the grey already.

'Do you miss home, Mum?' I asked her as we were walking back to our little house.

'This is our home now, Leelu,' she said. 'You'll feel different in a few weeks' time. There's just been so much to adjust to.'

'How long will it be before Dad comes?' I asked. Mum and Dad had both become very good at dodging this question, I'd noticed.

'Oh, you know, when his work thing is wrapped up, he'll be here right away, I'm sure.'

'But how long will it take for the work thing to finish? How many more days?'

'Oh,' said Mum. 'It won't be too lo— Tiber! Come back!'

All of a sudden Tiber had jogged into the middle of the road and bent down to pick something up.

'What were you thinking? Picking old rubbish up off the street!' Mum asked as he ran back, leaping lightly onto the pavement beside us.

'I found a phone,' he said, holding up an old, battered mobile. 'Now we can call Dad.'

Mum looked at him doubtfully. 'Someone must have dropped it. We should hand it in.'

'Come on, Mum,' said Tiber. 'We can't hand it in around here. It looks like it might be broken.

Someone probably just threw it away. People do that on this street. You know that.'

Mum hesitated. 'Well, if it's broken, what do you want with it?'

'I'm sure I can fix it,' Tiber said. 'Anyway, I may as well try rather than leaving it in the road to get run over.'

He smiled convincingly. I'd often seen him do this with Mum and Dad when he wanted his way. I've got to say it usually worked.

'Well, all right,' Mum said. 'I suppose it can't hurt. But if you find something on there that tells you who it belongs to, then we need to try and find them and give it back. OK?'

'OK,' Tiber said. His eyes were wide, he looked very innocent, but I saw him crossing two fingers discreetly behind his back.

We carried on walking, but this time Tiber was bent over the old phone, taking the back off, examining the battery.

Later, when we were getting ready for bed, I asked him if he really thought he could fix the phone.

'Of course I can, Lulu. It'll be easy. We'll be talking to Dad before you know it,' he said. 'You believe in me, don't you?'

I shrugged a little but nodded. I wanted to believe that Tiber could do it, although he had been trying to fix it all evening and hadn't got very far.

That night, when Tiber was snoring in that funny whistling way he does when he's deeply asleep, I looked at the moon. It wasn't full, just a tiny toenail clipping of a moon. I couldn't see the crater. But I thought hard about Tiber fixing the phone.

Let Tiber fix the phone, I thought. *Let Tiber fix the phone.* And then: *Let Tiber fix the phone so we can talk to Dad.*

Over and over, until the words seemed to blend together.

And then I had a thought: I reached for the thing I had found in between the bin and the lamppost and clasped it tightly in my hand.

Once again I thought I felt a slight movement, but I had to admit that I wasn't sure it had really happened.

I held it with a clenched fist and thought again: *Please let Tiber fix the phone. Please let Tiber fix the phone. Please let us be able to talk to Dad. Let me hear his voice and know that he's all right.*

This time there was a definite quiver.

I quickly looked over at Tiber, who was snoring in the other bed, and the phone that lay beside him. Tiber's fingers were still touching it; he had been playing with it right up to the moment he fell asleep.

Nothing about the phone, or the thing, seemed to have changed, and in the end I fell asleep thinking that perhaps I'd imagined the walnut changing the coin toss; perhaps I hadn't felt those things move on my palm.

Perhaps there was no such thing as magic or powers, just the plain old world in front of us and nothing more to it.

7

'Leelu! It's Dad! Dad's on the phone!'

I tried to shake the fogginess from my head but it refused to shift, hanging in my mind, suspended and still.

'Tiber did it,' Mum said with a grin.

'I told you I'd fix it!' Tiber said. His smile was even wider than Mum's.

'We'll leave you to it, shall we?' Mum said. She shut the door behind them.

Through the little holes at the top of the phone I could distantly hear Dad's voice. He was saying my name. I grabbed hold of it.

'Dad?' I heard myself say. I still felt a bit drowsy and disbelieving, but that was what woke me – the sound of my voice, which didn't sound so sleep-ridden after all but normal, alert and bright.

'Leelu?' came Dad's voice from the small black plastic phone.

'It worked,' I whispered, remembering last night. In spite of all my doubts, it had worked.

'Leelu, are you there? I can't hear you. Leelu?'

Dad was the one who'd first called me Leelu. The smudged printed writing on my birth certificate reads *Lillian Elvira Olawale*, but no one calls me that. When I was very small, Tiber couldn't say 'Lillian' properly, so Dad had just come out with it one day. Since then, it had stuck.

It's always *Leelu this* and *Leelu that*. Tiber calls me Lulu sometimes, usually when he wants something, but mostly it's just Leelu.

'I'm here, Dad!'

'Leelu!' he shouted down the phone to me. He laughed. His chuckling made my heart swell. It made me think of bubbles trickling into the air, leaves dancing in the wind. 'How are you?'

His voice sounded so tiny, so very far away. I found it hard to imagine that the words from the phone were actually coming out of the mouth on the dear round face I knew so well.

'We miss you – when are you coming?'

'I'm working on it, Leelu.'

'Where are you?' I asked. I wanted to picture him. Even though we'd only been away a few days, I felt as though my home was being washed out of my mind by the grey of London.

'I'm at home,' he said.

'Where? In which room?'

'Just in the kitchen. It's a beautiful day. The sun's pouring through the windows; everything is waking up.'

I closed my eyes, and for a moment I wasn't sitting on my lumpy mattress in London any more; I was back at home, in our old kitchen. I could smell the sunshine in the air; it smelled of promise, and of beginnings. I could hear the old sounds as clearly as if I was back there.

'Are the birds singing?'

'Yes, the birds are singing.'

'Is the generator humming?'

'Mmm,' Dad said.

'I wish I was there with you, Dad,' I said, but he changed the subject.

'Tell me about London.'

Just then, a siren started up outside. I heard someone shouting something; it pierced the air angrily. The sound of that voice, so hard, so sharp, seemed to suit the weather here, so unforgiving and cold.

'What's your room like?' Dad asked when I didn't answer him.

'It's . . .' I started to say, looking around. Tiber's and my things were jumbled together in piles. We hadn't brought much with us, but it seemed like there was a lot in here already.

'Messy,' I finished.

Dad chuckled again. 'Well, you'd better tidy it up then, Leelu.'

I didn't tell him that I couldn't get comfortable in our new bedroom, that I couldn't sleep through the night without waking and wondering where I was. That in those dark early hours of the morning I remembered that we had left home and that Dad wasn't with us, and it stopped me from getting back to sleep. I turned over and over on my creaky, wheezy bed and thought of my old bedroom; I wished I was there.

For starters, I didn't have to share with Tiber in our old house. I had my own room. I could shut the door behind me and not have to worry about Tiber steaming in, teasing and tormenting.

Before I came along my bedroom had been Dad's study and he'd had to move his desk downstairs. It wasn't huge. In fact, there was only just enough space for my bed, a wardrobe, a chest of drawers and little else, but to me it felt cosy. Dad called it my little cave.

It had once been the room where he'd sat at his old, scarred desk and done his work. 'This is where you can make things happen,' he said to me, slapping the top of his desk and the papers that were scattered across it.

I felt myself missing my old house; it was like a physical pain, a stab through the heart. Mum kept telling me that it was the people, not the place, that made a home, but I wasn't sure she was right. I thought you needed both.

'Dad, when are you coming? I miss you.'

'Not—' Dad started to say, but then the line began to crackle and his voice was lost in static.

'Dad! Dad!' I called out. 'Can you hear me?'

I caught flashes of his voice. Then parts of words that sounded like a robot was speaking them.

'Dad! Don't go!'

I suddenly had an idea. I pulled up the loose floorboard and reached for the walnut that lay underneath it.

Just as I had done before, I held it tightly in my hand. Wishing with all my might.

Please don't let the phone call end.

Please don't let Dad's voice disappear.

Please keep us connected.

But this time the walnut didn't move at all.

I thought I heard Dad saying my name in a robotic drone.

'Dad, don't go,' I heard myself say aloud.

But I could barely make out the words he was saying any more; it was as though they had been cut into pieces and then stuck together again in the wrong order. And then, suddenly, one word rang out clearly through all the fuzz. For one moment I heard Dad again.

'Help,' he said, and then his voice dissolved into fragments.

I squeezed the walnut so tightly that my hand began to hurt, but still it didn't move.

The phone went very quiet.

When I looked at the screen, I saw that the call had ended.

Dad was gone.

8

After my phone call to Dad, I rushed downstairs
to find Mum and Tiber. They were pushing
spoonfuls of soggy-looking cereal, a greyish mush,
into their mouths as though they were robots.

'I think Dad's in trouble,' I told them
breathlessly. That made them drop their spoons
with a bang.

'What happened?' Mum said as Tiber grabbed
the phone from me, furiously pressing the buttons.

'We got cut off, but before that I heard him
say, "Help," like he was in trouble or something.'

Tiber looked up from the phone. 'I can't get
through to him.'

'There's no need to worry,' Mum said, standing
up. 'That happens with phones all the time. You
just had a bad connection. Did his voice go a bit
funny – like unclear?'

'Yes, but—'

'You can't hear what people are saying when that happens,' Mum said. 'I'm sure he's fine.'

'But—'

'There's no need to worry,' she said again with a hard stare that made my lips fasten to one other. 'Put it out of your mind. We'll speak to him again soon. For now, we need to think about getting you ready for school tomorrow.'

Mum had sounded very certain, but a little later I noticed her picking up the phone and trying to make a call. When there was no answer, she put it back down again, her forehead creased with worry.

The day dragged by, although there were lots of things we needed to do. Mum took us to a shop with clothes balanced in precarious piles, and made us try on trousers, jumpers and T-shirts. They were all grey, of course. The hard shade of the roads.

I couldn't understand why, when I tried to keep the call from Dad going, the walnut hadn't worked; I kept looking outside to see if anything else had been left by the bin. If I did find something else, I could wish that Dad would ring us back. But the space remained empty for the rest of the day.

9

Tiber walked just ahead of me on my first day of school.

I tried to catch up with him, but he simply extended his long legs effortlessly, lengthening his stride, so he was always, always just out of my reach, a few steps in front.

'Hold hands when you cross the road,' Mum had told us the night before. She would still be at work when we woke up in the morning because her job went on right through the night. She was going to work in one of the big clothes shops, and during the night she had to put everything out, ready for the morning shoppers. But she promised me she would be there to pick me up from school at the end of the day.

'Tiber, you listening to me? You must hold Leelu's hand crossing that busy road.'

'YesMum.' Tiber said it so fast that it sounded like one word.

But when we approached the busy road, Tiber was still ahead of me and I had to half walk, half run to keep up with him.

The cars seemed angry. They either stampeded past us in a blur or sat in unmoving lines, impatient, sounding their horns. The smell of petrol made my head hurt and I wanted to be somewhere else.

'The road, Tiber.' I found it hard to speak because I was trying to keep up, and my words were lost in the roar of traffic. I was sure he hadn't heard me.

In my pocket I felt for the old, wrinkly conker I had found that morning. I'd spotted it in the space between the bin and lamppost as soon as we left the house, and I'd managed to shove it into my pocket while Tiber was locking the door.

A red bus came steaming past. It churned through the air, making me feel very small, my flesh and bones insubstantial and flimsy.

'Mum said . . .' I tried again, but Tiber had speeded up once more. I broke into a run on the hard pavement and the plastic bag with my lunch in it knocked against my leg painfully.

'Tib—'

But then he spun round with the grace of a dancer and, with a darting look both ways, he took my hand and pulled me across the road through a tiny gap between the cars that existed only for seconds.

We arrived on the other side as the traffic closed behind us, and he dropped my hand just as swiftly as he'd taken it.

He was ahead of me, just like before.

And I had to run to catch up.

I heard the other children before I saw them.

There were shouts. A light, happy bumble of chatter. As I heard those sounds, I felt my own voice binding itself up, coiling tightly within my throat. I knew that if I opened my mouth to speak, no words would come out.

'Your class must be over there,' Tiber told me, gesturing towards a group of children who looked roughly the same size as me.

'I don't know,' I said. I looked at the other children in the playground, and their voices seemed to get louder. My ears rang with their shouts and screams. The sounds rattled through my head as though I was quite empty, full of echoes.

There were too many differences between us.

I was as still as they were fast, sprinting, running, skipping, filling the space.

I was as silent as they were loud, shrieking in their game of tag.

I was as alone as they were tangled in their friendships. I thought I could see the connections between them, shimmering in faint lines, like spiders' webs in the air, tying them to one another.

I took a few small steps towards the children that Tiber had pointed out, but there seemed to be a huge expanse of playground between us.

There were as many mothers and fathers there as there were kids. They stood a little way off, but their gazes kept returning to their children. Their faces were dominated by watchful, devoted eyes.

The sound of them filled my head too. They laughed easily. They chatted and joked. They spoke in that loud sort of way that showed they didn't care who overheard them. Now and again they'd break off to call out their child's name, their voices turning into a shriek, a warning. *Mya! Abbie! Shai!* It sounded not unlike the sirens that flooded the busy roads outside.

I felt a fluttering in my chest, something beating as though it wanted to escape. My breaths came quickly but I couldn't take in a proper lungful of air. My mind started to reach out for something that would steady me, but everything seemed to be revolving. Or was I the one who was revolving and everything else was staying still?

I stuffed my hands into my pockets and slouched a little, making myself smaller. My fingers closed tightly around the hard shape of the conker. I thought I felt it shift in my fingers, making the smallest of movements.

With closed eyes, I imagined Dad standing in the playground.

I wished that he was there with me, taking me to my new school.

When I opened my eyes again, I thought I saw him. Just a little distance away from me, talking to the other parents, standing and smiling and *being Dad*.

His eyes darted towards mine now and again, checking in with me; where I was, how I was doing.

As I saw him there, I found I could suddenly take in a full breath of air again. I felt my chest loosen and my shoulders relax. I hadn't realized that I'd been holding them so tensely.

Among the hum of talk I heard Dad's light chuckle. It rose above the chatting and shouting, and carried in the wind around me. When he laughed like that, his eyes lit up as though a fire was burning inside him, fierce, bright and true. Now, through the parents, I saw his profile. The round of his belly, the snub of his nose. The way he rested one hand upon his tummy if he was laughing, as though trying to contain it.

I ran towards him, darting in between the groups of parents, the bags and pushchairs. Dad was here! He had come over after all. Did Mum even know, or had she been in on the surprise?

I was only a few metres away from him, my hand outstretched. In just a few more steps I would be able to touch him.

Then I heard the hard, sharp sound of a whistle being blown and the children dispersed into long, winding lines. Their parents clucked around them, putting them in their places, handing over lunch boxes, school bags and kisses.

In the bustle, Dad had vanished.

10

'Come on, Leelu,' Tiber said, gesturing towards the children he'd pointed out before. 'Get over there!'

But I didn't move. Or couldn't.

I was standing alone, some distance from the lines they had formed, and for a moment I wondered if I could actually become invisible.

Thinking of everything that I had already made happen with the walnut and the ridgy wooden thing, I wondered if I might really be able to do it.

I thought hard. I clenched the conker again.

I pictured myself very, very small.

My toes were facing inwards, and then my feet turned more and more in on themselves, my shoulders slumping downwards ... until I could no longer be seen.

It felt as though it was working.

For a moment I wondered what the day that lay in front of me would look like if I did become invisible. The children would disappear into the school, the parents would make their way home, and there I would stand, silently, until the playground was quite empty.

I would go down the slide first, I decided. As many times as I wanted. Now that there was no queue.

Tiber's voice broke into my dreams.

'Leelu, come on. Quit playing around – open your eyes. Stop being so weird.'

I opened my eyes to see him looking at me, slightly puzzled.

'Why did you close your eyes?'

When I didn't reply, he made a sort of huff of annoyance, like a dragon expelling smoke.

'Well, never mind that now – go over to that line. I'm going to be late.'

'I can't,' I admitted.

I thought Tiber might start to get cross with me. I heard him take a deep breath as though he was getting ready to shout. I braced myself, but when he spoke, his voice was soft. So quiet that I could barely hear him.

'It's going to be OK,' he said. He came over and ducked down so we looked each other directly in the eye. 'Let me tell you a secret.'

He looked around as though to check that no one was listening. 'I'm feeling scared about my first day too, Lulu.' His eyes changed for a moment; they softened, widened. Not often does he ever look afraid of anything. It took me a moment to realize that this was what his eyes were telling me.

'But we'll make friends,' he said. He was trying to sound convincing but his voice seemed just a note too high. 'We both will. It'll be easy, you'll see.'

'But what if—' I started to say, but then one of the mothers came marching towards us. Tiber straightened abruptly, and when I looked up at him, his expression changed again to one of indifference. Boredom, almost. The children had started to plod inside now, still in their wonky-looking lines, and people had begun to stare at us. I wasn't with them, I wasn't in the right place, wasn't doing the right thing.

'Hiya!' said the mother. She waved at us like she knew us, like we were old friends. When Mum meets new people, she looks at them hard, her mouth fixed in a rigid line. She says she's making her mind up about them. It takes her a long time to make her mind up about most people.

The mother in the playground smiled at us so widely that I could see she had little gaps between her front teeth. She was perhaps the same height as Mum but, with her shoulders back, arms swinging by her sides in a relaxed sort of way, with her bouncing stride, she seemed much taller.

'Just thought I'd see if you guys were OK over here,' she said. She spoke in a funny way that I hadn't heard before. Her voice went up and down all at once so everything sounded like a question.

'My sister is starting school today,' Tiber explained.

'Your first day, huh? I remember it from when we started here. We had no idea where to go. It's confusing, huh?' The words seemed to bound from her mouth.

I made my head nod, just a tiny bit.

'Ah! Well, welcome, welcome!' She knelt down so she was on my level. Her eyes reminded me of the sky at home in the morning, when the sun is shining and there's no suggestion of rain. 'My name's Catherine. What's yours?'

I didn't call adults I knew at home by their first name. My parents had taught me to be respectful, as was the way of our tribe, and I'd call adults 'Auntie' or 'Uncle'. Did she really want me to call her Catherine?

'Tell her your name, Leelu,' Tiber hissed.

I tried to say it in a normal way, but without meaning to, I whispered it.

'OK, Lou,' said Catherine. 'Shall we find out what class you are in? What do you say? I can show you where the office is, if you like.'

'I need to go, Leelu,' Tiber said. 'Will you be all right?'

Again I gave a tiny nod.

Quite unexpectedly he reached down and hugged me quickly. I felt the strength of him through his skinny arms. I didn't want him to let go, but all of a sudden I was released and he turned away. I watched him stalk out of the playground with long, giraffe-like strides, until he was gone.

'You have a nice brother,' Catherine said. 'I have two boys and they seem to spend the whole time wrestling each other into headlocks.'

I followed her through one of the doors and we walked along a corridor to the school office. There was a smell in the air which seemed both familiar and not. I couldn't work out what it was, but I think it was something cooking.

'Here it is,' Catherine said to me. We'd reached a long desk that had a glass panel all along the top; it reminded me of a cage. 'Mrs Charlton will know what to do. Why don't you sit down on one of those chairs?'

The fabric on the seat felt scratchy and pricked my bare skin. I saw Catherine talking to a lady who sat behind the glass and they both looked over. Catherine smiled at me again reassuringly, but the lady behind the glass frowned a little.

'All right, Lou? Mrs Charlton is going to take you to meet your new class. Just wait here, OK? It was nice to meet you.'

I said, 'Nice-to-meet-you-too,' very, very quietly, and then, more quietly still, 'Catherine.' I wasn't sure she'd be able to hear me, but she winked at me and said, 'Nice manners,' and 'Catch you later.'

She gave me another one of her gappy-toothed grins and was gone.

When Catherine left, I was very aware that I really was alone. Somehow she'd made me not feel that way when Tiber walked off. I had the feeling that I was trapped there, sitting on that scratchy chair. Not in a normal way, not like being locked in a cupboard, or surrounded in a corner; I felt like I was trapped in my own body. I couldn't move, I didn't want to move. I didn't want anyone to notice me.

A sensation of heat, a burning, rose from the base of my spine. It filled my head, hung around my neck and ears. It made me feel stiff and unwieldy, as though I was becoming rusty and cumbersome like an abandoned car.

I could hear phones ringing, children chatting in the corridor, all the sounds of school life continuing around me. They got louder and louder, those sounds, until my ears burned with them. And then suddenly there was a sharp *tap, tap, tap*, and everything was a normal volume again.

It came again: *tap, tap, tap*. Insistent and cross. I moved my head ever so slightly in the direction of the sound, and then I saw that it was Mrs Charlton who was making the noise. She was using a pen to rap on the glass in front of the desk.

'Yes, you,' she said. She beckoned me over, wielding her pen as though it was a baton. As soon as I started to approach, she looked away and her eyes locked onto her computer screen. She did not look at me again.

'What's your name?' she said. She typed loudly on the keyboard, and the sound made me think of her rapping her pen against the glass.

'Leelu,' I said.

'Leelu?' Mrs Charlton squawked. 'I haven't got a Leelu down here.' She leaned towards the computer screen, her eyes narrowed. 'Only a Lillian.'

'That's my other name,' I said quietly.

'Are you Lillian or not?'

In the end I said, 'Yes,' in a small voice.

'Right, now we're getting somewhere. Michael! Michael! Come here,' she shouted to a boy who was walking past, so loudly that I couldn't stop myself from flinching.

'Take this girl to Class Fourteen. Tell Mrs Winters she's just arrived and I've registered her.'

The boy nodded and disappeared out of the room.

Mrs Charlton continued to type. Without looking up she said, 'Go with him, then.'

I ran out into the corridor and saw Michael just as he was turning a corner. I thought he might speak to me, but he walked on in silence while I trotted alongside. He finally stopped in front of one of the doors and knocked three times.

We heard someone shout, 'Come in,' and Michael opened the door, repeated Mrs Charlton's message and abruptly left. I stood there in the doorway, and suddenly I found I couldn't move my feet.

There was a large group of children sitting on the carpet. They all turned their heads to look over at me.

Pairs and pairs of eyes before me.

They seemed to be looking right at me, but their stares also streamed through me somehow; as though I was a pane of glass, transparent and thin.

'Come in, come in,' the teacher said. She smiled warmly, but it made me feel uneasy; I remembered my old teacher from home, who never smiled. Her face was held immobile by a glare that would silence everyone in the class without her having to say a word.

'Would you like to come and sit down over here?' my new teacher said, pointing to a little space. 'We've just started Literacy.'

I wasn't sure what Literacy was, but I forced my feet to move and walked slowly towards the space she had indicated.

'I'm Mrs Winters. It's Lillian, isn't it?'

'Leelu,' I said. Some of the boys tittered.

'Leila?' my teacher asked.

'Leelu,' I said again. The titter was louder this time.

'Settle down,' Mrs Winters said. 'Quiet! Quiet!' But the laughter didn't subside for a few moments, even when she shot a meaningful stare at some of the quaking shoulders.

'Well, come and sit down,' she said eventually, and then she quickly muttered a word under her breath that sounded a bit like Leila and Leelu rolled into one.

I sat down in the space, which was so small that I had to tuck my legs beneath me awkwardly. Then I saw Mrs Winters frown slightly and I looked around. Everyone else was sitting with their legs crossed, their knees pointing out at sharp angles. I quickly copied them, and Mrs Winters nodded her head ever so slightly in approval and looked away.

I wish I could say that was the only mistake I made that day.

But it was just the beginning.

11

'How was school?' Mum said as I ran over to her. She was waiting in the playground as she'd promised. She stood a little bit away from the other parents. Their heads were dipped in conversation whereas Mum was stifling a yawn. She was wearing a brown cardigan and hugged her arms around herself as though she was cold.

I didn't speak. I pressed my head into her body so she couldn't see my face. She smelled so familiar. Like a day at home when the earth is baked by the sun. A hint of spice from cooking up a stew. And something else, something indescribable: the scent that was just her. For a moment I imagined that we were back in our old house with Dad. London was just a faraway, nondescript place that I had heard other people talking about.

'You must be Leila's mother. I'm Mrs Winters,' I heard my teacher say. 'Have you got time for a quick word?'

'Yeah, sure,' Mum said. She barked the words as though she was cross. She pushed me away from her stiffly and looked at Mrs Winters through narrowed eyes, her lips pursed. 'Leelu, go and play over there while I talk to your teacher.'

I was reluctant to leave her, but I walked away a little and stood by a wall that had been painted to look like a forest.

I saw Catherine picking up her two sons. They ran around her, excited, delighted, in circles. She noticed me standing there and gave me a thumbs-up, a bright smile. I tried to smile back but my face felt like it had become stiff, frozen. I'm not sure it would have looked like I was smiling.

'Hope you had a good day, Lou!' she called out to me – but then one of her sons ran into the other and they both started crying.

I looked back over at Mum and Mrs Winters. Mum was standing very straight, staring at Mrs Winters fiercely. The grim line of her mouth seemed to set, become permanent and rigid. Her eyes flamed. She opened her mouth and I thought she was going to shout, but she thought better of it and dropped her head, defeated. When she looked back up at Mrs Winters, her eyes seemed empty, expressionless. She nodded a few times, little curt movements, but did not speak.

I walked up behind them to see if I could hear what they were talking about, but Mum noticed me. She quickly ended the conversation and turned to tell me we were going now.

'Is everything OK?' I asked her once we were walking down the road away from the school and were no longer surrounded by other children.

'Well . . .' she said.

'What did Mrs Winters say to you?'

'She said . . . She said . . .' But Mum didn't seem to want to tell me.

'Did I do something wrong?' I asked.

'No,' she said firmly. 'Nothing you did was wrong, Leelu.'

'Did some of the other children in class say something about me?'

'No – why would they do that? What would they have to say about you?' Mum asked.

I was sure the other children were talking about me behind my back. I stuck out somehow, even though all I wanted to do was fit in.

Dad always said that if people said something about you, it was actually more about *them*.

It was always after dinner that he started talking about things like this. When we were all round the table together.

'Listen up, kids. This is important,' he'd say. 'If someone says something nasty about you, it's because there is something about themselves that they don't like.'

'That doesn't make any sense,' I said. 'Why would they do that?'

'The thing is,' Dad said, 'they don't even realize they are doing it. They have no idea. But, mark my words, it's always about them really. Not you. You are just caught up in it – you just got in the way.'

In spite of Dad's words, I still felt sick at the thought of everyone talking about me behind my back. I reached into my pocket for the conker I'd found and squeezed it hard. Somehow, just doing that took my mind off the tears I could feel building.

'It's just . . . It's just . . .' Mum started to say, but then she thought better of it. 'Well, it will be OK. It'll just take time, huh? You're a quick learner. You'll soon catch up with everyone. You'll get used to it.'

I nodded, and Mum looked relieved. She squeezed my hand and gazed up at the sky where, for a moment, the sun's rays beat down, warming us.

How could I tell her that I didn't think I ever would?

12

All day at school I'd felt like everyone was speaking a different language.

Mrs Winters asked questions about things that I had never heard of. There were words everywhere. Words I didn't understand, words I had never heard of before. They were on different coloured cards covered in shiny plastic, plastered all over the classroom walls. They even covered up the glass of some of the windows, blocking out the light.

The worst thing was, I was the only one who couldn't follow. Everyone else in the class seemed to know the answers. They chanted them as casually as saying hello or goodbye. My mind was racing, trying to listen, to understand. I could feel myself leaning forward, straining to catch up with what I couldn't follow. At times I felt that I was beginning to grasp what Mrs Winters was saying, but then she'd veer off in a different direction. She talked quickly, and showed us pictures and sentences on the whiteboard that flashed before us at an alarming speed.

When it came down to doing the work, I had no idea what I needed to write. Instead of sitting there doing nothing though, I filled the pages with any word I could think of. I even copied some of the longer ones that were on the walls. I kept my handwriting neat: each letter the same size as all the others. When Mrs Winters came round and saw the page of writing I'd completed, she smiled, but as she read it, her face fell.

'OK, I think that's enough for today. Good try,' she said. Her voice sounded flat, a little dull. 'Why don't you go and choose a book from the book corner and have a read for the rest of the lesson?' She took my writing book and turned away.

I nodded and carefully put away my pencil and tucked in my chair while everyone else in the class carried on writing. I felt their eyes on me again, as I had when I'd first walked in that morning. It seemed to take a really long time to walk from where I was sitting to the book corner; it was as though everyone's stares had made my legs slow down.

When I got there, I sat down behind a shelf on one of the cushions that were scattered on the floor, so no one could see me.

I realized that someone, Mrs Winters probably, had tried to make the book corner comfortable and nice, and it was maybe this that made me feel even more upset. I couldn't really explain it, but sitting on the nice cushions, on the brightly coloured rug with the pile of blankets that felt soft between my fingers, I felt worse than when I was sitting on the hard plastic chair at the table, trying to do work I didn't understand.

I peeked over the top of the bookshelf. All the other children were still scribbling away, lost in their own world of words, and Mrs Winters was reading something at her desk, frowning a little.

Just then the classroom door opened and Louise, the teaching assistant Mrs Winters had introduced me to earlier who works with our class, came in carrying several piles of paper.

I watched Mrs Winters beckon Louise over. She said something to her and handed her whatever it was she was reading. I saw immediately that it was the new writing book she'd given me that morning, the one I had just been working in.

Louise stared at my book, her eyes scanning the page, and then looked back at Mrs Winters. They both began to laugh. I could see that they were trying to stop; they looked away from one another, and Louise even clamped one hand firmly over her mouth. But it was too late. The wisps of their laughter carried across the classroom to me and whipped across my face like a slap.

I wished I could be anywhere else but there. I wished, as I had in the playground, that I could make myself invisible and slip away from this classroom without anyone's eyes on me. I remembered seeing Dad in the playground. For those few moments he really seemed like he was there. I felt sure that *I* had done that. That, once again, by using one of the things I'd found by the bin, I had somehow found a power to make things happen.

Could I do it again?

I reached into my pocket for the hard, shiny conker and squeezed it tightly.

Please let me be somewhere else, I thought. *Please let me not be here.*

The conker didn't move, and so I tried again. I squeezed it harder, and closed my eyes.

Please, please, please, I thought. *Please let me leave, with no one seeing me go, no one stopping me.*

But it didn't twitch; nothing changed around me.

It hadn't worked.

I couldn't understand why, so I clung on tighter still, and this time I whispered it: *Please get me out of here. Turn me invisible. Please, anywhere but here.*

Just then I heard someone stifling a giggle, and when I opened my eyes, one of the boys – I learned later that his name was Drew – was looking over the bookshelf at me.

'What are you doing?' he said. His eyes were wide with embarrassment. But not for himself; for me.

I couldn't answer him. My mouth opened but nothing came out, and then, out of nowhere, I felt tears building behind my eyes. They gathered there and began to fall.

'Are you . . . ? Are you . . . ?' stuttered Drew, and then he turned away abruptly and I heard the sharp hiss of a whisper. I didn't need to peek over the bookshelf to know that he had told everyone on his table what he had seen me doing.

I turned quickly and, without looking, picked out a book and pretended to read, fiercely wiping my tears away. I tried to concentrate on the words on the page but they seemed to swim in front of me. Moving, floating almost, just out of reach.

'Leila?' Mrs Winters said.

I looked up at her. I didn't bother correcting her.

'What are you reading there?'

I shrugged and showed her the cover.

'Are you enjoying it?'

I shrugged again and pretended to keep reading.

'Can you read it to me?' Mrs Winters asked.

I stared down at the words in front of me and concentrated hard. I knew that this was what people looked like when they were reading – I had seen them do it.

'Maybe you could start from here,' Mrs Winters said, and pointed to one of the words. '*The next best thing* . . .'

'*The next best thing*,' I said. '*The next best thing* . . .' I stuttered, and then fell silent. I could feel tears growing behind my eyes again.

I tried once more. '*The next best thing* . . . *is* . . . *to* . . .' but after that I lost my place and couldn't find it again.

'OK,' said Mrs Winters quickly. 'Maybe you'd like me to read some to you?'

I nodded, and handed the book to her and concentrated on not letting myself cry. I gritted my teeth, swallowed hard.

'*The next best thing is to look at the spokes and the metallic hawsers of the Eye itself,*' Mrs Winters read. I couldn't follow the story, but the sound of her voice was comforting somehow. I focused on the words on the page and I didn't cry again.

Mrs Winters didn't ask me to do anything else that day.

13

When I got back that afternoon, I noticed something new stuffed between the lamppost and the bin.

As soon as I spotted it I ran over, able to forget for a moment all that had happened at school that day. I shrugged off the stiffness I felt from the cold wind that had buffeted us on the walk back and made me long for the warmth of home. I missed the feeling of heat in your bones that you carried with you throughout the day there.

This thing looked different from the other items; only when I got closer did I realize that it was a matchbox. I plucked it out and shook it, but it didn't rattle with matches. I thought it might be empty; it felt light in my hand. But before I got the chance to open it, Mum called over to me.

'Leelu, don't hang around that bin. Come inside, away from there.'

I quickly stuffed it in my pocket, out of sight.

*

'How's school, Lulu?' Tiber probed as soon as he walked in, a little later. He dumped his bag on the chair, and in one fluid movement leaped up to sit on the work surface.

I didn't answer him.

'That bad?' He leaned in towards me. He smelled a bit like smoke mixed with what the rubbish by the bin smelled of, and his eyes, like before, looked wide, worried. I thought it might be one of those rare times when he said something comforting and kind or private, just between the two of us, but at just that moment Mum walked in.

She turfed him off the work surface with a 'Get down from there!' and as he leaped, she sniffed the air. She started spraying a can of air freshener around. It smelled cloying and artificial; its sweetness made my head swim.

I wondered how Tiber's day at school had gone, but I didn't want to ask him. That way, I wouldn't have to explain about mine.

'Is Dad ringing us tonight?' I asked instead. I felt I might have been able to tell him what happened today; he might have had an idea for how to make it better.

'I'm not sure,' Mum said. She was distracted, sorting through the pile of dirty clothes that had mounted in the corner. 'I don't think so.'

I carried the day with me for the rest of the evening. It was a heaviness that weighed down on my shoulders. I'd always known that I wasn't especially good at reading and writing. Sometimes, when I stared at a page, it was as though the words were shifting around. At other times it was as if they had turned into balloons; they rose up off the page and floated away, out of my reach.

At my school back home I'd never felt that I was behind everyone else. I thought that I would get better in time; that it would just take me a bit longer than the others. It hadn't even bothered me much.

Now I knew that there was a huge gap between me and everyone else. I felt it as a problem that poked and prodded and needled me, and would not leave me alone. The thought of returning to school started to make me feel sick. A little burrow in my stomach flipped with nerves at what the next day might bring, at how I would cope when I was asked to do something I did not understand.

The only thing that distracted me was the matchbox. I wondered again who had left it there and why they had done so. I wondered whether I could make something happen with it, as I had done with the walnut and the wooden thing and the conker. I remembered the coin toss and the broken mobile phone and Dad appearing in the playground. I'd made those things happen – I was sure of it. By holding those things in my hand and thinking hard about what I wanted, I'd changed the way things were going to be.

It hadn't worked every time, of course. I hadn't been able to make myself invisible. I hadn't made myself disappear in the classroom. For some reason the things didn't always work, and something told me that I shouldn't try and use them for something small, just to test them out. I understood – as clearly as I knew that singing in the morning would irritate Tiber – that I should only use the things when I truly needed them.

All through the evening I kept reaching into my pocket to enclose the matchbox within my palm, exploring its corners and edges, wondering, wondering what it might contain, and what I might be able to do with this new thing. It was as I was running my fingers over the matchbox that I heard a crash outside, in our small concrete square of a garden.

Mum was showering upstairs and Tiber was in our bedroom, supposedly doing homework. I walked slowly over to the back door and peered out through the glass. There was no one there, but a ball, grey with dirt and scuffed around the edges, rolled slowly across the concrete and then finally came to a stop just in front of me.

Then I heard yells and shouts from the Noisy Neighbours' garden, and then a face, with two large brown eyes that seemed to glow and grow larger as I looked at them, appeared over the wall. Then an elbow, an arm, two legs and the rest of her body flew over the wall as though it had been thrown over, like she was a ball herself.

It was the girl I'd seen crossing the road the other day. The fearless one who had darted out to get the football and speeded away from the car, only just in time.

She landed lightly on the concrete with her knees bent, and looked around.

For one absurd moment I wanted to hide. I retreated and thought about ducking down behind the sofa so she couldn't see me. But by then the girl had already spotted me. She pressed her face against the glass of the door, using her hands to shade her eyes, and when she saw me, she started to wave frantically, beckoning me over.

'Hi,' she said with a huge grin when I opened the door. She was tiny. She must have only reached my shoulders, but the way she stood made her seem about the same size or even taller. Her hair was very short and tufty, sticking up at angles; even brushing it wouldn't make it any neater.

'Hi,' I said back shyly, unable to quite meet the gaze of her large brown eyes.

She pointed to her chest with her thumb, prodding herself roughly, almost punching herself, and said, 'Betsy. I'm Betsy.'

'Leelu,' I said quietly.

'Huh?' she said. 'What's that?'

I tried again. A little louder this time. 'Leelu – I'm Leelu.'

'Ah – hi, Leelu.' She reached out her hand to shake mine, something no one I'd met had ever done before. We shook hands vigorously. 'I'm sorry, I apologize. We kick our ball over and I come to get.' She shrugged her shoulders over at the ball.

'It's OK,' I said. 'We don't mind. We don't use the garden much.'

'You just move here?' Betsy asked.

'Yes, not long ago. Although it feels like we've been here ages already.'

'It's like that when you move. Everything new. Everything to get used to. It speed time up. Makes you tired.'

'Yes,' I said. That was exactly how it was.

'I go now,' Betsy said. She did something with her feet that made the ball spring up into the air.

She caught it neatly and tucked it under her arm. She turned to leave, but then stopped and turned back to me. 'You play?' she asked, gesturing to the ball.

I shook my head.

'I teach you,' Betsy said, and then she threw the ball high over the wall and there was a cheer and a scrabbling sound. And then Betsy herself scaled the side wall, vaulted over into her garden and was gone.

And in the empty yard, for the first time that day, I felt myself smile.

14

It was only much later, when Mum had kissed me goodnight and left for work, when Tiber was in the bathroom having a shower, that I dared to open the matchbox.

The cardboard was very old and worn, but I could still make out the faded picture of a ship on the front. It was sailing across ornate blue curls for waves. I slid the drawer out.

Inside there was a clump of something yellowy green; some sort of plant that reminded me of a sponge, the way it clung together. It had a dried-out feel but was still soft to touch, like the fur of a cat or the doughy rug that we kept in the bathroom.

I handled it for a while, passing it from one hand to the other, enjoying its lightness. When I heard the shower being turned off, I quickly scooped it back into the matchbox and hid it beneath the floorboard alongside the other things I had collected.

It left fragments of green and brown on my palms, which I flicked onto the carpet so there was not a trace left. I buried my hands beneath my duvet as I settled into bed.

When Tiber came back in, I felt my secret as though it was something burning. To me it was fierce, blazing, almost uncontrollable. I was sure that if Tiber saw me, he would know just by looking at my face that I had something to hide. I concentrated on staying quite still so he would think I was asleep, but my mind was whirring furiously, turning everything over. I wondered how sure I really was that the things gave me powers or whether I had just imagined they did.

I heard Tiber take a few steps towards me, and concentrated on keeping my breathing even and deep. It seemed like a long time before I heard him walk away. Then I heard him slowly opening the wardrobe door, delicately pulling out drawers. I sensed that he was trying not to make any noise, that he was trying not to wake me, which struck me as odd because Tiber usually enjoyed doing things like that.

After that the bedroom door closed. I heard his muffled footsteps creeping slowly down the stairs. And then the unmistakable sound of our thin blue door being slammed shut.

I threw my duvet off and looked around the bedroom, half wondering if this was just a practical joke that Tiber was playing on me; perhaps he would jump out from behind one of the empty suitcases that were piled up in the corner.

There was no sign of him.

15

'Tiber?' I said aloud, cautiously at first and then louder, and louder still. 'Tiber? Tiber?'

There was no answer.

I didn't need to go downstairs to know that I was alone, but I went into each room anyway.

Without Mum cooking something on the stove or Tiber wandering around distractedly, tapping on his phone, each room felt alien to me.

It was more than the rooms just being empty.

It was like I had never been into them before.

There was so little of us in these rooms. Our things were all here of course; our clothes and bits, a couple of framed pictures of Dad and us together, open packets of food we had eaten. But there were no happy memories made here, no stories that these walls could tell. As I looked around at our scattered belongings, it was as if we were only staying here for a night or two, passing through on our way to somewhere more permanent. It didn't seem possible that this was now the place we called home.

I shuffled back upstairs to my bed. Although I felt sure that sleep wouldn't come, I felt more secure there somehow. I arranged my duvet around me like a fort, plumping up my pillow so that I could sit up comfortably to look out of the window. And then I waited, I watched. Waiting for Tiber's return.

I looked up to see if I could find the moon. The sky outside was orangey, not really dark because of the light from the streetlamp. It was a very different sky to the one I knew from home, where darkness fell like a curtain, very quickly, very suddenly, densely black and obscuring all the light.

There was no sign of the moon tonight. I looked at the road instead. It was empty, but after a little while I wondered if I could see things in the shadows. Darting movements. Figures in the blackness. Though when I tried to look for them, they seemed to disappear into the darkness as though they had never been there at all.

At first I wondered if this was all Tiber; joking around, thinking it was funny to dance in the shadows, teasing me. But another part of me doubted that even my brother was capable of such a drawn-out joke.

I felt myself spiking with the unfairness of Tiber leaving me all alone in this strange house. Dad had spoken about treating each other as we would want to be treated ourselves. I couldn't help thinking that I would never have left Tiber alone by himself here, because I wouldn't want him to do the same to me.

In the end I stopped looking for him.

My gaze rested on the lamppost and the bin.

A piece of furniture had been dismantled and left there, leaning against the bin. Boxes were stacked with what looked like bricks and pieces of rubble, piled up and abandoned. A broken umbrella poked out at an angle.

But among it all, my eyes were drawn to that little sliver of space between the lamppost and the bin.

I thought that, if I waited long enough, I might see the person who had been leaving things there.

I watched two boys walk past very slowly, but they didn't stop. Another couple shoved some rubbish into the bin, but after they had hurried on nothing had been left in that space.

For a very long time no one else came. I stared out at the empty street and the shadows until the pavement started to merge into the road, the lamppost into the bin, trees into sky. I was falling asleep. My eyes were beginning to weigh down and close, but just then I saw a flicker of movement outside, something darting across the street in a rush, which made me sit up, rouse myself so I could see what it was.

It was a dog. It ran out in circles across the road, its huge grey head swinging from the ground to the air, trying to catch a scent of something. I recognized it as the one from the house next door, and sure enough, I saw the old man shuffle into view.

I don't think I made a sound or anything like that. I didn't have the light on and I was sitting very still, but at that moment the old man stopped.

He straightened as if he had noticed something, and then, all of a sudden, he looked up.

Right towards my window.

Right at me.

16

I dived down under my duvet and pulled it over my head. I tucked my body underneath so there was not a single part of me showing.

My eyes were closed tightly. Even though it was impossible for anyone to see me through the window now, I kept absolutely still.

I was too afraid to look out again.

Lying there in the darkness, wishing for Tiber, wishing for Mum, wishing I wasn't all alone, I felt completely helpless. There was nothing I could do, nowhere I could go, no one who could help.

I thought for a moment about small, fearless Betsy from next door.

She wouldn't hide under the bedcovers.

She wouldn't be scared.

She would tell herself that the door was locked, that she was safe. That it had just been a coincidence, the old man looking up at the window.

I stepped out of bed tentatively, making the loose floorboard squeak beneath me, and thought of all the things I had stowed there.

That was it!

I pulled up the floorboard and reached for the matchbox. I carefully fished out the contents, and held it enclosed in one hand. I didn't squeeze it tight as I had the other things because it was so delicate, but I felt the usual little shift, a twitch of movement. I knew it would work.

Let Tiber come back, let Tiber be safe. Let Tiber come back, let Tiber be safe.

I hadn't even thought it three times before I heard the sound of a key in the front door and then the steady jog of his steps coming up the stairs.

As he came into our bedroom, I flicked on my lamp. 'Where've you been?' I demanded.

For a moment Tiber looked surprised, shocked, even ashamed to see me, and then his features rearranged themselves and his expression changed to one of indifference. He shrugged his shoulders and, ignoring me, kicked off his shoes and threw his jacket onto the end of his bed.

'Tiber, you just . . . you just . . . left me. I didn't know what had happened. When Mum finds ou—'

'But Mum isn't going to find out, is she?'

'But—'

'Leelu, don't make this into such a big deal. I came back, didn't I? Everything's just the same as it was. Don't say anything to Mum, OK?'

'But, Tiber, you know it wasn't—'

'Look, I won't do it again, all right? But please don't tell Mum.'

'You promise?' I asked. 'You promise you won't leave me alone again?'

'Of course,' Tiber said. His face looked like he was telling the truth – his eyes were wide, with nothing to hide – but I realized I couldn't see his hands. I remembered the way he crossed his fingers when he was making Mum a promise he didn't want to keep.

'Show me your hands and say it,' I said.

Tiber huffed, but he did as I asked, splaying his fingers out wide in front of him. 'I promise I won't leave you alone again.'

'All right,' I said. 'I won't tell Mum. Or Dad,' I added.

'Great. Can we go to bed now?'

'I suppose so,' I said.

I couldn't fall asleep though. I tossed and turned, and as soon as I started to drift off, some noise, whether outside or inside me, woke me. Each time I checked that Tiber was still there. He was oblivious to my worries: he started snoring almost as soon as his head hit the pillow and slept heavily through the night.

The next morning he was up before me, eating breakfast, showing no signs of having been out late the night before. There was a dull but persistent ache in my head. I didn't know if it was from lack of sleep or something else.

It was only as I slowly trudged to school, my head thudding painfully, that I remembered, like a weight bearing down on me, the man from next door last night. The way he had looked up, straight at our bedroom, and seen me at the window.

However much I tried to convince myself, I felt that somehow he had known I was there – although there was nothing to give me away; no light, no sound, no movement.

How could he have known? The thought made me feel uneasy. I remembered his dog's great head, swinging down to the ground and up again, and shivered.

When Mum picked me up from school that day and asked me how I was, I said with a forced smile that I was fine. She didn't question me further and I didn't tell her anything about the night before.

That evening, as he had promised, Tiber didn't leave the house. He seemed unsettled and prowled around, unable to be still for long. In the end he took up residence on the sofa, stretching across the whole length so there was no room for me. I went up to our bedroom.

I took up my usual post at the window.

The evening had not yet faded to night. I looked down the street, my eyes immediately going to the space between the bin and the lamppost, as they always did. There was nothing there, so I contented myself with looking at everything else. A breeze blew through the trees, making the leaves sound like rushing water. Just then there was a burst of movement from the house next door. I saw Betsy out front, this time without her gaggle of brothers. She dashed up to our front door and knocked three times. Her small fist made a surprisingly loud noise that echoed through the house.

I flew downstairs and, before Tiber had risen from the sofa, flung open the door.

'Hi, little fish,' she said when she saw me.

'Little fish?'

'That's what I call you. Because that's what we're like. Little fish in big pond.' She gestured at the buildings that surrounded us on every side.

Back home, there were spaces that seemed to go on for ever; you could walk and walk and never see a building, or a car, or a wall.

Here, there were walls everywhere. Grey lines drawn all around, cornering you, trapping you into tight spaces.

'Hi, other little fish,' I said back.

Betsy started laughing. It was a deep gurgle of a laugh. 'I come round to see if you want to play football tomorrow. After school. My dad will be out, and so tomorrow we play.'

'Why does your dad have to be out?'

Betsy waved her hand in the air as though batting away a fly. 'Tell you another time.'

'Yes, sure. I won't be very good – I'm not good at—'

'That's why we play,' Betsy said simply. 'OK, I go now, little fish.'

'Bye, other little fish.'

She gave another gurgle-laugh and left.

If Betsy hadn't come round that night, I probably wouldn't have seen it. From my bedroom window I didn't have quite the right angle.

At the bottom of the little space between the lamppost and the bin there was a small package. It was wrapped in newspaper and tied with string in a loopy-looking bow. It must have fallen down and was now lying on the ground, almost obscured by a bag of empty beer cans.

Another gift.

17

'It was so real!' Dad said. 'I really thought I was there with you.'

Dad had told me there had been nothing wrong after we had last spoke, just that his phone had cut out. He said I must have imagined him calling for help.

Everything was back to normal. Well, as normal as it could be when he was so far away from us. He was describing a dream he'd had to me. He used to do that in the old days, at home, only back then it would be over the breakfast table and he would be right in front of us, brandishing a spoon and a wide grin.

'You were wearing grey trousers and had a plastic bag with your lunch in it. And Tiber was there too. He was next to you. I was with the other parents, standing right by you.'

'Maybe it wasn't a dream, Dad,' I said.

'What's that, my love? You're breaking up a bit.'

'I said, maybe you really *were* there.'

'Well, it certainly felt like I was. It was very nice to see you and Tiber, even just in dreamland.'

I remembered wishing for Dad to be there with me as I held the conker in my hand in the playground. He was laughing with the other parents; I'd heard the sound of his chuckle – and then the whistle went and he had vanished.

'Were you laughing in the dream?' I asked.

'Well, now that you mention it, I was. How did you know?'

'Because you're always laughing, Dad,' I told him. He began to chuckle. I'd missed that sound; I felt my heart grow bigger just hearing it.

'Now tell me, Leelu, how's school going? Are you doing OK?'

Dad always asked questions I didn't want him to ask. I knew that if Mum asked me something, I could distract her, but not Dad. He would always sense if you were avoiding the question.

I was saved by Tiber coming in and demanding to speak to Dad. I didn't want to tell him that things hadn't got any better at school, but I knew that, if Tiber hadn't come along, I'd have ended up admitting it. Dad had a way of always extracting the truth of how you felt.

At school I was trying very hard to do the right

thing, but it was difficult when I wasn't sure what that was exactly.

'Why don't you speak?' one of the girls in my class said to me one day. She was called Terri.

I opened my mouth to answer, but then I realized that I didn't know what to say, so I closed it again.

'She never speaks,' said Aisha, who wore her hair scraped back from her face in a high, dramatic ponytail. She looked thoughtful. 'I'm not sure if she knows how.'

'Oh,' said Terri. She frowned at first, but then she nodded as though she had understood something, and walked away from me.

For some reason I couldn't blurt out that at my old school I'd talked all the time. That I'd once even got in trouble for chatting too much; Dad had given me one of his talks about not distracting other people from their work.

Despite what Tiber had told me on my first day, I didn't make friends at school.

For him, it was a different story. He spent most of his time on the mobile, not trying to ring Dad but sending messages to his new friends. I gave up trying to talk to him because he was always bent over the small screen, his fingers tapping the buttons, only responsive to its beeps and vibrations.

He hadn't left at night again, but sometimes he came back well after school had finished. He'd say something like, 'Homework club was on,' or 'There was an after-school talk,' but from the way he tilted his head to the side and the bright gleam in his eyes, I was pretty sure he was lying. But Mum never questioned him and I wondered if I'd got it wrong.

He did seem a little more distant on those days though. His eyes were never still; they didn't settle on anything. And he seemed more agitated, like the house wasn't big enough for him any more. Sometimes he smelled of smoke, like car exhausts. And I noticed that he always took a shower when he came in. But I didn't think about it too much really. I had my own worries.

At school I was more and more alone. Whenever one of the other children smiled at me or asked me something, Terri or Aisha or one of the other girls would quickly explain that I didn't speak, that I didn't know how, that they shouldn't bother talking to me. I was left well alone – because who wanted to speak to someone who wouldn't talk back?

I grew quieter and quieter – until one day I realized that I hadn't spoken at all at school apart from saying 'Yes, miss' almost silently to the register in the morning. Mrs Winters never pushed me to say it louder, and for that I was grateful.

She'd look over at me with large eyes, but she didn't urge me to speak up or chide me for being too quiet as she did with the other kids.

When Mum asked me about my day, as she always did, I told her that it had gone fine and she would pinch my cheek gently, affectionately, like she used to when I was little. She would never ask me anything more, as Dad would have, and so I said nothing more.

I never lost the feeling of loneliness that had begun on that first day, sitting outside Mrs Charlton's office on that scratchy blue chair. Nor the feeling of being watched. I felt like people were always looking at me; they could see how alone I was. It was as though I had a line drawn around me that no one wanted to cross.

No one but Betsy.

'You got to speak,' she would say to me. 'Speak up! No mumbling!'

We'd got into the habit of spending the afternoons together. Betsy went to another school that was a bus ride away. When her family first came to this country, they had lived in another part of the city and she'd started at a different school, and her dad didn't want to move her.

'My voice just clenches up and I can't say anything,' I tried to explain.

'How can voice clench up?' Betsy said, her head cocked to one side, which I knew by now meant that she was thinking about something.

'It's too late now,' I told her. 'Everyone thinks I can't speak. Even my teacher. She won't ask me a question any more because she's worried I won't say anything and there will be silence. Which there probably will be because I don't know the answer anyway.'

I knew from the first that I could confide in Betsy. She knew all about Dad not coming with us; how Tiber had changed since we'd arrived; everything that had happened at school.

She in turn told me what it was like to have so many brothers who were always shouting and fighting. How she missed Colombia and her cousins who still lived there. She had adjusted to the cold weather by keeping moving and by wearing two T-shirts under her jumper.

Betsy told me a little more about her family. She didn't seem to like talking about them that much. Her dad worked nights like Mum, but at the hospital. Sometimes he got so angry that he was controlled by his anger. She made it sound like his anger was quite separate to him; a person who sometimes came to visit and was unwelcome but who insisted on staying over for a while anyway.

'My mum left for long time now,' Betsy said with a shrug. 'She didn't like my father being angry also.'

'I'm sorry,' I said immediately.

She shrugged again. 'It's the way it is. She was scared.'

But Betsy wasn't scared of her dad; she wasn't scared of anybody.

She was a good listener, though she was also good at calling a halt to conversations when there was nothing more to say.

'Let's play now,' Betsy said, as she so often did when she deemed that we had, in her own words, 'done enough talking'. 'Today we shoot on goal.' She nodded to herself at the suggestion.

Betsy thought the answer to most things was football, and when I first told her about my troubles at school, she'd immediately said, 'I definitely teach you football. It make everything much, much better.'

I had my doubts about that, but in fact she was right: I always felt better after we had played together, even though I wasn't particularly good at football.

But I could only see Betsy for those few hours after school. The rest of the time I was very, very lonely. I always stowed one of the things I'd found by the bin in my pocket. Mostly it was the walnut, but sometimes it was the wooden, ridgy thing, or the matchbox. The last surprise – the package that had been carefully wrapped in newspaper – was some sort of dark green, dried-out leaf. I couldn't carry that in my pocket or it would have fallen apart. I always left it in my hiding place under the floorboard.

I had figured out a little more about how these things worked. I could only use them once. After that they were used up. So I stowed my leaf away very carefully. I would use it only when I really, really needed it.

Although the other things wouldn't work any more, having them in my pocket made me feel a little less lonely somehow. Someone was leaving those things for me; someone who knew that I needed them, knew that I would like them. So, I supposed, I did have friends after all. I had Betsy. And someone else too; someone I had never met.

Just as I got used to not talking, I got used to being alone at school. It wasn't so difficult in class because we had to be quiet in lessons, but, unlike everyone else, I didn't look forward to playtimes.

I felt much more alone when I was surrounded by all the other children, playing, shouting to one another, running past me as though I was invisible.

I started to dread going to school. My feet dragged along more and more slowly each morning. One day Tiber was annoyed with me for making him late, and started to pull me along by the hand.

It hurt, but he said it was my fault. He told me I would get used to going to school here. *He* had, hadn't he?

But I wasn't so sure I would.

18

One morning, though, Mrs Winters came over during Literacy and said that she wanted me to spend some time with a different teacher.

The new teacher met me outside the classroom. She had very long brown hair that snaked down her back, and a friendly smile. Around her neck she wore a large pendant – a bright blue-green stone – and through her nostril, the shiny curve of a nose ring. When she spoke to me, she bent right down so that her face was level with mine.

'Hello,' she said. She looked genuinely pleased to see me, as if we had met before. Like the mother in the playground, Catherine; like Betsy in the garden. 'I'm Ms Doyle. How do I say your name?'

I whispered it, but because she was so close to me, she heard me and said, 'Leelu! Am I saying it right? That's a lovely name. Leelu, Leelu.' I think she liked saying it out loud; she kept repeating it.

'Leelu, right. What we're going to do is visit my room today. I have all sorts of things in there that I think you might like. Do you want to do that?'

I nodded.

'Let's go, then,' she said. She held out her hand and when I took it, I felt the edges of her silver rings. They held large, bluish stones that caught the light.

'I like your rings,' I said quietly. Again, I wasn't sure if she would hear me, but she beamed down at me and said, 'They're called moonstones. On my rings. They look a little like the moon, don't they?'

We came to a very narrow staircase. 'It's best to run up here if you can,' Ms Doyle said and, with that, sprang lightly up the steps ahead of me. The stairs bent round and round, so when I turned each corner I wondered if she might have disappeared.

'There, we made it.' Ms Doyle pushed open a door and beckoned me in.

Her room was full of stuff. The ceiling was draped with scarves; the shelves were full of interesting things. Pictures covered every available space. It didn't feel like I was in school any more but in some sort of treasure chest, where the light was pink and blue and yellow. On one table there were all sorts of animals. On another was a box full of puppets. On every bit of wall hung photographs or bookshelves with books of all shapes and sizes.

I didn't know where to look first.

'Would you like some water, Leelu?' Ms Doyle asked me, and poured me a cup before I could answer. 'There's a lot to do up here, but today we are just going to have an explore. Sound good?'

I nodded. While I was looking around, I saw something I recognized on what Ms Doyle called the 'nature table'. It was just like the stuff I'd found in the matchbox.

'I have some of this,' I told her.

'Moss?'

'Moss,' I said, repeating the word.

'It's great stuff, isn't it?' Ms Doyle said, and passed her clump of moss from hand to hand in much the same way as I had mine when I first found it. 'It's so soft. I found this little piece in the woods near where I live. It had completely covered the ground. Where did you find yours?'

'I just found it in the street,' I said. I couldn't help sounding a little sad because the truth was, since I'd found the leaf wrapped in newspaper, nothing else had appeared. For some reason the person had stopped leaving things.

'Moss can grow in most places, especially on walls,' Ms Doyle said. 'We could have a moss hunt, if you like.'

I nodded, and then I spied something else on the nature table that I knew. 'Miss Doyle?'

'Oh, you say my name like "mizz". Like a bee. Mizz Doyle.' She buzzed a bit more and laughed. 'What have you noticed, Leelu?'

'I have one of these too. But my one looks a bit different to this.' I pointed to another object. It was like the wooden thing I'd found after my first day at school; the thing I didn't know the name of.

'A pine cone. They grow on pine trees. Do you know what a pine tree looks like?'

Ms Doyle reached up for a big book, which she flicked through. 'Here we are,' she said, showing me a picture of a huge, towering tree with a shaggy mass of leaves; it came to a point at the top.

I looked at the other things on the table. There weren't any walnuts, but one of the leaves looked like the one I'd found wrapped up in newspaper and tied with string like it was a present. The last surprise.

'What's this?' I asked.

'That's just a little piece of bracken. It's beautiful, isn't it? I love the shape.'

I nodded in agreement. I hadn't used my piece of bracken to do anything yet – though I was sure that I'd be able to make something happen with it if I wanted to.

'So, Leelu, is this your favourite part of my room? The nature table?' Ms Doyle asked me.

I nodded. 'I like . . .' I started to say, but I was so unused to speaking at school that the words stuck somewhere in my throat. I didn't finish the sentence.

But Ms Doyle smiled warmly and looked at me as though she was carefully considering what I was saying – and I felt my chest loosen. I felt able to speak.

'I like these things,' I said, and gestured to the bracken and the moss and the pine cone that I'd placed around me in a circle. Then, all of a sudden, words came bubbling out of me. 'A friend used to give me things like this. They were like . . . treasure. But now they've stopped and I don't know why.'

'Have you asked them why?' Ms Doyle said gently.

I shook my head.

'Well, maybe you could give them something back. Have you tried that?'

'That's a good idea,' I said.

Ms Doyle looked at her watch. 'Gosh, Leelu, it's time to get you back to your class already. But we'll meet again. In two days' time. On Friday. OK? Maybe you would like to bring in some of the things your friend has given you? Sounds like you are quite the collector.'

My face fell at the thought of going back to the classroom. Ms Doyle went quiet for a moment when she noticed. She looked like she was thinking. Her nose ring twinkled in the light.

'Why don't you choose one of the things from the nature table?' she suggested. 'To give to your friend?'

'Really?' I said. 'I can take something?'

'Yes, of course. What would you like to take? What do you think they might like?'

I looked from piece to piece, and in the end I took a little bit of what Ms Doyle told me was bark from a silver birch tree. It felt a bit like paper and was white with brown markings.

For the first time since I'd come to school, I felt myself begin to relax.

I tucked the silver birch bark carefully in between the pages of my reading book so it wouldn't get damaged in my bag, and smiled.

I hoped that the friend I had never met would like it.

19

The day after I met Ms Doyle, Betsy and I were sitting on the patch of scrubby grass across the road from our houses. Betsy had told me last week that she and her family were going back to Colombia for a couple of weeks but I'd tried not to think about it.

Though I knew that she would come back, two weeks without her felt like a long time.

It was the last afternoon we had together before she left.

The ground beneath us felt cold and we had to keep getting up and running around and stamping our feet to keep warm. I remembered my home, where the earth was baked by the sun and radiated into the soles of your feet. The heat eased into your limbs and your bones, so you never felt truly cold.

'I go get the football,' Betsy said, and at that moment her brothers burst out of her house, calling out and jostling one another, the football on the ground in front of them.

'Hey,' Betsy shouted out to them. She stood up, lifting her shoulders and straightening her back so that she was as tall as she could possibly be. 'It's our turn now.'

'You had your go, Betsy. You had it yesterday,' one of the taller boys said.

Betsy had told me their names: Miguel, Juan, Alejandro, David, Diego, Pedro. But I couldn't tell them apart.

'Hey!' Betsy shrieked, and sprinted over to them. Even though she was much smaller than them, she was louder. The boys flinched a little as she shouted. 'My turn. Me and Leelu. We are cold.'

One of the shorter boys, who was holding the football, looked as though he was going to hand it over.

'No, Pedro,' the tall one said, and stood in front of him. 'Betsy, you and your little friend can't have it. You can play with us if you want to, but you can't have it all to yourself.'

In a flash Betsy had turned towards me, her eyebrows raised and questioning. I gave the tiniest shake of my head. I didn't mind playing football with Betsy but I definitely didn't want to do it in front of all her brothers.

'Next time it's ours,' Betsy said to the tall one, and though she was only half his size, she prodded him in the chest; the force of it made him take a step back. Her brothers ran off, a blur of bodies.

Betsy ran back and sat down beside me once more, a little deflated. She sighed loudly.

'You can play without me,' I suggested. 'I don't mind.' If it wasn't for me, she would be playing football with her brothers.

'No, little fish,' Betsy said straight away. 'I stay with you. Little fish stay together.'

She smiled over at me, a crooked sort of grin. Suddenly I didn't feel so cold any more, and in that moment I knew that I wanted to tell Betsy everything. All that had happened with the walnut and the pine cone, the moss and the conker. How I had found them and what they had allowed me to do.

'Betsy, I have to tell you something. It's a secret.'

'I won't tell,' she said immediately.

'I've been finding things. Just over there.' I pointed to the bin.

'Rubbish?'

'No, not rubbish. Someone has put things there on purpose, I think, so I would find them.'

'What things?' Betsy asked, crinkling up her nose.

'Things that give you powers,' I said.

'Powers?'

'I know it doesn't sound real but I swear it's true. The thing might look quite ordinary. A walnut, a conker. But they make you able to do things.'

'What you saying, little fish?' Betsy said. 'Magic?'

'Well, yes. It *is* magic, I suppose. I know it sounds crazy, but honestly, each time I wanted something to happen I held them in my hand and it did.'

I described to her the coin toss when we first moved in; the way the walnut had moved in my hand. How using the pine cone had fixed the broken mobile phone, the conker had made Dad appear in the playground and the moss had made Tiber return the night I was all alone.

'Every time it's worked.'

'So you can make something happen right now, if you want?' Betsy's eyes gleamed. She stood up expectantly, slapping her hands against her thighs.

'Well, no. I realized that I can only use each thing once. It gives you just enough power to change one thing. You can't keep using it over and over. And I only have the leaf left now. I haven't found any more things.'

'So the mystery person stop leaving you things?'

'Yes,' I said. It had been several weeks since the last gift. 'I don't know why, but I'm going to leave something there so whoever it is knows that I haven't forgotten them. Then maybe they'll start up again. I'm going to do it tomorrow when Mum's not around.'

'Show me exactly where you find the things.'

We walked over to the bins. My bin had collected some odd pieces of foam and an old dusty computer that looked like a tower block. Just as I was gesturing to the spot in between the bin and the lamppost, Betsy's grandmother, Maria, came out and called her in for dinner.

'Bye then, little fish,' Betsy said. 'Until we meet again.'

'Bye. Have a good time in Colombia.' My voice sounded very small, like when I'd tried to talk on my first day at school.

Betsy suddenly launched herself at me in a hug. 'I miss you,' she whispered fiercely into my ear, and then she turned and ran towards her house.

'Betsy!' I shouted out. She turned her head. 'I'll miss you too. Don't forget me, other little fish.'

'Never!' Betsy said. She grinned crookedly, and then disappeared into her house.

That night I took the piece of silver birch bark out of my reading book. It had got flattened and a bit cracked but it was still in one piece.

The next morning I put the bark in a carrier bag and carefully wedged it into the slot before Tiber came out.

I thought about it all day at school. I wondered again who was leaving things for me there and whether they would find my gift. Whether they would like it. And I thought about Betsy too, travelling back to her home country, the distance between us getting greater and greater with every moment that passed. I finished school and I wondered where she was then.

Mum was waiting for me as usual and I pulled her towards our house eagerly.

'What's the rush, Leelu? Why are you in such a hurry?' she asked.

When we turned into our street, I sprinted over to the bins, but I could see immediately that the silver birch bark had been taken.

20

Mum was in a rush to cook dinner.

'I have to do some extra hours,' she said, and glared at the packet of rice she'd taken from the cupboard, as though she could cook it with her angry stare alone.

'I can do it, Ma,' Tiber said. "You get off to work.'

'What's your game?' she said, and narrowed her eyes suspiciously. It's not like Tiber to help in the kitchen. He can be helpful with things like fixing the phone or getting the television to work or changing batteries. But not so much with cooking.

'I can do it,' he assured her, and started to light the gas with the little clicky thing that you have to point at the hob – just the way Mum does.

'Are you sure?' she asked, but she was already putting on her jacket and edging towards the door. 'There's some cooked chicken in the fridge to go with it. If I run now, I can catch the bus and I won't be too late.'

'We'll be fine – right, Lulu?' Tiber said.

I felt uneasy about Mum going, but she looked at me in such an expectant way that I nodded. Her face relaxed and she grabbed her bag and slung it over her shoulder in a final sort of way.

When the door slammed behind Mum, Tiber called out to me. 'Come on, Leelu, you've got to do your bit too. Watch this pot. If it starts to boil over, turn the heat down here, OK? And then, when all the water is gone, turn it off.'

'Where are you going?'

'I'll be back in a minute. Just going to pop to the shops. Get us some Cokes to have with dinner. Sound good?'

'Why don't we go together when the rice is done?'

'Nah, nah – I'll go now, and then, by the time I get back, the rice will be ready.' Tiber gave me one of his winning smiles, his head cocked to one side, eyebrows raised as if to say, *Now tell me that's not a good idea.* He turned and, before I knew it, he was gone.

I watched the rice carefully, just as Tiber had told me, and turned the heat down as far as it would go when the pot started to spit and splutter. It still kept shaking the lid though. It was like there was something inside that was trying to escape.

In no time, all the water had gone and the rice had plumped up, filling the pan. I turned the gas off as Tiber had instructed, but I thought I might have got it a bit wrong because there was a smell of burning. Tiber was still not back.

I looked out of the window; I even opened the front door to peer out, but the street was quite empty.

I imagined Tiber coming back. He'd say, 'Where's the plates, Lulu? Come on, come on. I'm ready to eat,' and he would throw down some cans of Coke. I started to serve the food so that everything would be ready when he came back. I couldn't find a big spoon to get the rice out of the pan, so it took a long time to put it on our plates. Then I found the chicken in the fridge and I put a piece for each of us next to our pile of rice.

Still Tiber wasn't back.

He didn't come back when the rice had gone cold.

He didn't come back when it started to get dark.

He didn't come back.

Any courage I'd felt slowly leaked away. I didn't know what to do. I thought about going out and trying to find him, but I didn't know which shop he'd gone to. I wondered whether to call Mum at work, but when I looked for the mobile phone, I couldn't find it. I realized that I didn't know the number to call anyway.

There was nothing I could do but wait and hope.

When it got darker still, I turned on all the lights. It made me feel a bit better, flicking on each switch and seeing every room light up. I climbed onto my bed and looked out to see if I could spot the moon, hoping to find the crater that Dad had pointed out to me. It was about my bedtime; the time he said he would be looking at it, but I couldn't see it. It must have been covered by cloud.

My stomach rumbled but I didn't want to eat my chicken and rice until Tiber was back. And the front door remained stubbornly closed.

Then I heard a sound. It was like something ripping. It was so loud it filled the house.

Next there was a flash of lightning; it made everything go white, and then, when I heard the rumble of thunder again, all the lights went out.

There was the sound of rain pouring from the sky as though someone had pulled a lever. It pounded against the windows as though it might break them.

When Tiber left the house, he hadn't been carrying an umbrella or wearing a coat, so wherever he was, he would be getting very, very wet.

The thunder came again. *Boom. Boom. Boom.* Each clap was getting louder, like footsteps coming closer.

The lightning flickered, piercing the darkness with its whiteness. It felt like the lightning and the thunder were in competition with each other, trying to see which could scare me more.

Then I remembered something Tiber had told me about lightning striking a building and killing the people inside. A fork of lightning, all sharp angles and jagged corners, filled the sky, and I began to shake uncontrollably. The walls of the sitting room flashed white and seemed to tremble.

I had to leave.

21

I ran out of the front door.

Immediately the rain drenched my hair and clothes. They were plastered to my skin.

'Tiber!' I shouted out loudly, but as I did so, I heard another sound behind me.

A metallic *click*.

The sound of the front door shutting.

I looked round, although it was hard to keep my eyes open in the pouring rain. I went back to the thin blue door and tried to open it, just in case it hadn't closed properly, but it didn't budge. I didn't have a key.

The rain soaked through my jumper. Coldness swept through me. The rain seemed to pound down harder than ever.

I looked around for shelter, but the trees were waving wildly in the storm. The lightning flashed again, illuminating their shaking branches, which looked like mighty arms that could sweep down and pluck me from the ground.

The rain lashed at the black windows of all the houses in the row. I wished Betsy was here, but her house was silent. Just looking at it made me feel more alone.

Once again the thunder started to tear through the sky above me, like something was being ripped in two. After it had finished I could still hear its vibrations in the air – but there was something else as well. Something softer than the thunder; something that continued after the rumble had died away.

It sounded like crying, although it didn't sound entirely human.

The lightning started up again. For one dizzying moment the whole street was lit up and then, just as quickly, plummeted back into darkness.

There was the sound of something slamming. I turned round and saw one of the front doors being flung open with such force that it banged against the wall.

It was the door to the house where the old man with the wolfish dog lived; the man who'd seen me at the window, the first night Tiber had left me.

He was standing in the doorway, oblivious to the storm and the rain that was drenching him. There was a faint glow of light behind him, but it was not bright enough to see his face.

A new kind of coldness surged through me now, taking root in my stomach, fixing my legs to the ground. My body didn't feel like it was my own any more. I wondered if my skin would crumple and fall to the ground like a coat I'd shaken off, after which there would be nothing left of me. Only fear.

I remembered all the times Mum had warned me about strangers; she'd told me I mustn't trust anyone. I couldn't stop thinking of Tiber's scary stories, which had stopped me from sleeping. Why was there always a storm in them?

I realized that I had no place to go, nowhere to hide; that there was nowhere to run but further down the dark street.

I glanced at the old man out of the corner of my eye. I couldn't see him clearly – there was a shadow across his face – but he had a blank sort of expression that made me wonder if he even knew I was there. I stayed absolutely still just in case he hadn't noticed me.

I felt sure that something terrible was about to happen. I closed my eyes. I thought of Mum and

Dad and Tiber and all the good things in my life. I remembered the feeling of a new morning back at home, lying in my bed in the room I'd grown up in, the sunlight pouring down from the blue of the sky. Stretched out across the mattress, lazing in the still part of the dawn, I heard the rise and fall of Mum and Dad's voices, making each other laugh. It struck me then that this was the nicest sound in the world and I wondered if I would ever hear it again. I thought of Dad's chuckle; the way it bubbled up out of nowhere and turned into shaking laughter that rocked his whole body.

The old man might reach out, I thought. *He might grab me.*

I felt my shoulders quiver, waiting for that moment to come.

But the moment passed.

Nothing happened. He didn't come.

When I turned back to the doorway, I saw that he was standing with his hands upturned, his face tilted towards the rain as though he was speaking to the sky.

'And there'll be no more of your rumbles, thank you berry much,' he said.

Something about his voice calmed me. It reminded me of sunshine, somehow; sunshine from back home, streaming down from the sky like ribbons. And the smell of Mum's sweet-potato stew. It made me think of Betsy and Ms Doyle and Dad, all mixed into one. The way he had spoken made me think of a song, the sounds bouncing up and down and fitting together to make something more than they could by themselves.

The old man looked up to the sky once more. And then he turned away, back inside, and was gone.

The door had been left wide open.

The rain, beating down harder than ever, made me step towards it. The hallway was softly lit, dry and empty.

As I got closer still, I heard something faintly in the air. It whispered down the hall towards me like smoke. Something like moaning, something like whining.

Then it faded and I heard only the violent pattering of the rain, the sweep of the tree branches as they were carried back and forth in the wind.

The thunder came again. It started quietly, and at first I wondered whether the storm had passed, but then it growled.

And then it roared.

As it died away, I heard the noise once more. A muffled cry.

'Hello?' I called down the hall.

There was no answer. No sign of the old man. There was just the soft light coming from the end of the hall, and in the semi-darkness I could see piles upon piles of things stacked on the floor. There were boxes and jars and bags full of things I couldn't make out clearly; when I stepped inside, I had to be careful where I put my feet.

I could still hear crying. Whatever it was whimpered and groaned, and hearing the sounds of something that was so clearly afraid made me less so. Over the crying I could also make out the broken words of the old man. They were oddly comforting and somehow familiar. His voice was tender and soft, as though he was singing a lullaby.

'Got you, I've got you,' he said, over and over.

I took a few more careful steps round the teetering stacks until I reached the room at the end of the hall. When I got there, I almost gasped aloud at what I saw.

Every part of the wall was covered. There were jars and jars and jars stacked one on top of the other to make a wall. Wooden boxes standing on their side that were stuffed so tightly that nothing fell out. There were feathers and branches hanging from the ceiling so that even I, small as I am, had to crouch in places. Among them hung jam jars holding nightlights. Their warm glow cast soft shadows across the floor.

I felt as though I had entered some sort of magical cave, rather than just a boxy, blank sitting room, which was what ours looked like.

And amidst all the junk the old man was opening jars and boxes and rummaging through them. He flung things out across the room. Diamond-grey feathers; pine cones of every size – one even skimmed past my nose.

He reached up onto the very tips of his toes and pulled out shoeboxes covered in thick layers of dust, emptying them onto the floor, and then pounced upon the innards, sifting through the odd assortment of stuff.

'Where is it, Dog, huh? I was sure I put it . . .'

Now and then he would break off his search and drop to the dog's side to stroke the huge grey head. The dog was crouched, legs tucked up underneath his body so that he looked smaller than I remembered. He was shaking, and with every clap of thunder he shuddered more violently.

It was the dog that was making the crying sounds.

'Now, now, Dog,' the old man crooned. 'I'm not far off. It'll only be a tick-tock, I'm sure.' He then leapt away as though he had springs inside him, and started on his frantic rummaging again.

There was another great rumble of thunder, the loudest I'd heard, and the dog shook violently and shrank down even more.

'Dog!' the old man cried, and immediately went over to calm the quivering creature. 'Don't worry, I won't let the storm in. I just won't open the door to it!'

He stroked the dog from the very top of his head, just above his eyes, all the way to his tail, over and over. The dog looked up at him gratefully and, with each touch, grew just a little bigger.

'Aha!' the old man exclaimed suddenly. He went to delve behind a stack of boxes and brought out an armful of tubes that, from the pictures on them, looked like they had once held crisps. He uncapped them and tipped them upside down. They were full of the same sort of moss I'd found in the matchbox by the bin.

He swept the whole lot up into a big ball, pressing it together, then closed his eyes. He was saying something, but I couldn't make out the words.

The ball of moss quivered, and then it shook violently. It looked like it was hard for the old man to keep hold of it, but when it stopped, there was silence around us.

The rain had stopped falling.
The wind had stopped howling.
The thunder had stopped thundering.
The storm was over.

22

'There we are!' The old man clapped his hands together delightedly and the ball of moss fell to the ground, discarded. 'Better, Dog?'

'You ... you ... you stopped the storm!' The words fell from my mouth.

'I did,' the old man said, looking right at me, his eyes twinkling as though he had known that I'd been standing there all along.

'And that's not all I can do, is it, Dog? But you know that already, don't you?' The last question he directed at me. His eyes reminded me of two very shiny conkers. They made brown seem like the best colour in the world. Rich and bright, warm but mysterious.

Suddenly I felt a glow, a warmth inside me. I knew something that I hadn't known just moments before.

The friend I didn't know . . .

The friend who had sent me powers when I needed them most . . .

My friend was standing right in front of me, picking off bits of moss and tasting the odd bit, and then wrinkling his nose in disgust.

'*You* left me those things.'

'Of course, a horse, of course. I left you those . . . wonders.'

'Wonders?'

'Come on, Dog. Something to settle your nines, I think.'

The old man disappeared into the kitchen and the dog stood up and stretched out, extending each leg. He was absolutely huge. When I first saw him out in the street, I'd refused to leave the house. Now, the dog loped up to me and bent his head. I reached out to stroke him, and only then did he leave the room and follow the old man into the kitchen.

'Splendid-diddly-o!' I heard the old man shout loudly.

They returned to the sitting room, the old man ducking round the branches hanging from the ceiling, moving this way and that as though walking through a maze. He began to collect the things he'd pulled out, staring at each piece intently and then stuffing it away in nooks and crannies in every part of the room. There was a system here, but I wouldn't have been able to tell you what it was.

'Dog does not like storms,' the old man said. Maybe to himself; maybe to me. Maybe to his dog.

'What's your dog's name?' I asked.

'Dog!' he exclaimed as though it was completely obvious and he couldn't believe I didn't know.

'Hey, Dog,' I said, and the dog stretched out at my feet with his nose resting on my shoe.

The old man was sorting pine cones into different sizes and shapes. Among them I spotted one similar to the one I'd found.

'Why did you leave me those things?' I asked him.

He was ignoring me again. He just carried on making his piles, and I thought he wasn't going to answer, but then he spoke. 'Why do we do anything? Because we need to, because someone else needs us to. Head, shoulders, needs and toes, needs and toes.'

Just then I heard footsteps outside.

Footsteps that flew and danced over the ground.

Footsteps that I knew.

It was Tiber returning at last.

'Home time,' the old man said, but when I looked at him, he was tipping the piles of cones into different-sized glass jars, screwing the lids on tightly and not paying me any attention at all.

I dithered; I knew I had to go but I didn't want to. 'Can I come back? On another day? Can I ask you about—'

'I told you,' the old man said, a little irritably now. 'Head, shoulders, needs and toes. If you need to come back, then . . .' He didn't finish his sentence, as though he had run out of patience with it.

I turned away from him and his dog and his collection of things, the overturned boxes and the flickering glow of the nightlights hanging overhead. Outside, I found Tiber opening our front door.

His eyes widened when he saw me. 'What are you doing out here?' he demanded, making me forget for a moment that he was the one who'd left me alone all night; I felt guilty for being outside.

I opened my mouth to object, but then Tiber said, 'I'll keep it from Mum. Just this once. She would be so mad if she knew that *you* had been out at this time of night.'

So I didn't tell him anything and I didn't find out where he had been either.

And I certainly didn't tell him about the old man and the dog from next door.

I didn't tell him how I'd seen the old man stop a storm.

23

'Some people!' Mum kissed her teeth as she saw a car draw up and someone dump more rubbish by the bin. 'I'm going to say something sooner or later. I'm sick of living like this.'

She said this all the time but she didn't really mean it. She carried on cooking her sweet-potato stew, but from time to time she stared out of the window towards the bin and the growing pile of rubbish around it.

Tiber was lying asleep on the sofa, stretched out long and thin like a pencil. I wasn't surprised that he was tired after being out for almost the whole night. Any time I tried to ask him where he'd been or why he'd left me, he would turn to me, his eyes dark. 'If you keep on, I'm going to tell Mum that you went out on your own.' So I stopped asking, although I didn't stop wondering.

'I didn't know anyone could sleep this much,' Mum said, and raised her eyebrows at Tiber, prone and still.

I didn't answer and looked at the wall on the other side of which I'd seen the old man and Dog. Among the piles and piles and jars and jars of things.

I had to see him again. I had so many questions for him. Where did he get the things from? How did they work? And, I wondered a little shyly, why had he left them out by the bin? Did he mean for me to find them?

For the next few days I didn't get my chance though. It was half-term, so Mum took a few days off work, and both Tiber and I stayed in. We had a Big Tidy of the house, which involved Mum chasing us around with sponges to scrub out sticky old cupboards that never looked properly clean. After that she said we should try and decorate a bit, but as we didn't have much money she asked Tiber and me to do some drawings to stick up. Tiber flat out refused, so I did as many as I could.

Later in the week Mum took us to find the local park, but it was surrounded by roads, the ground littered with cigarette ends. The grass grew scantily amidst patches of mud.

There was a sort of climbing frame, which Tiber and I tested out. Tiber hung upside down from the bars by his legs, then pulled himself back up and swung off easily. I couldn't do anything half as good as that, but when I managed to climb to the very, very top, I called out to Mum to look at me.

She didn't hear me at first; I could see her looking around at the cars, at the people sitting on the bench. Her face was set in lines. I thought I could see her tutting, just like she does when she sees the rubbish piled up by the bins. Then she heard me and managed to smile and clap at me. I waved at her very carefully and quickly, taking one hand off the bar.

Later on we got a phone call from Dad; it had been so long since we'd heard from him, and Tiber and I crowded around the phone, talking at the same time. He just laughed when he heard us babbling away.

'Let me speak to Mum first,' he said when he'd stopped chuckling.

Mum went off into the hallway so that we couldn't hear exactly what she was saying to Dad. We didn't need to be told not to follow her.

Tiber and I waited our turn. Tiber didn't say anything, but I knew that he was just as excited about talking to Dad as I was. He pretended that he was fiddling with his watch, but I saw the little smile that kept creeping up around the corners of his mouth.

Now and again Mum's voice would rise sharply and then fall, like it did when she was angry. Tiber knew the pattern too; he raised his eyebrows at me when she did it a third time. Then we couldn't hear her at all; I thought Dad must have been talking non-stop.

But when Mum came back, she didn't hold out the phone to either of us. 'He had to go,' she said. 'He'll call back soon.'

I didn't know what to say, but Tiber slammed his hands down on the work surface so that it rattled and shook. The sound of his hands slamming down – that was exactly how I felt.

'None of that!' Mum shouted, but Tiber quickly turned and raced out of the back door. I didn't know why he was going that way – that door only led to the tiny square of concrete that was our garden. It had walls all the way round. We hardly ever went out there because it smelled so bad.

'No you don't! No you don't!' Mum was yelling, and I turned just in time to see Tiber vault easily over the wall and disappear.

Mum ran outside but it was too late.

He was already gone, and by the time she ran out of the front door there was no sign of him.

24

'Stay right there, Leelu,' Mum told me, and she grabbed her handbag. She thrust her keys into my hand.

'Lock the door behind me with this key. See? Here. And only open it to me or Tiber. Do you understand?'

I took the keys and Mum ran out of the house. For a moment she paused as though unsure which way to go. She looked one way and then the other, and then she started sprinting the way we go as a shortcut to the shops.

I did as Mum said and locked the door behind her. There was also a thin-looking silver chain, and I put that on as well, although it didn't look very strong; it reminded me of a bracelet I used to have.

For a while I sat by the window in the sitting room. As each person passed I looked out for Mum and Tiber, but they didn't return. After a while I sat awkwardly on the sofa, feeling that I should be doing something yet not knowing what.

And then, as though drawn like a pin to a magnet, I picked up the keys Mum had given me, unlocked the door and took off the chain. I closed it quietly behind me and peered down the road. There was no sign of Mum, no sign of Tiber.

I suddenly wished that everything was different. I wished that Tiber hadn't run away and that Mum hadn't followed him. That I hadn't sneaked out of the house. That we were all together now, eating Mum's sweet-potato stew.

But that's not how things were, and when I looked one way down the street and then the other and still didn't see anyone, I headed towards the old man's house. I glanced at the bin – at the teetering bags of rubbish and the grey lamppost – but there was nothing slotted into the little space today.

I noticed that the door to the old man's house was even older and shabbier than ours. It was blue, just like ours, but it was much more faded, and the number 96 was brown with rust. I looked for a doorbell or knocker, but there was nothing like that so I just used my fist to knock.

There was no answer and I wondered if I hadn't done it loud enough; I knocked again. With much more force.

Rap, rap, rap.

I thought I heard someone moving around inside, but at that moment I heard voices down the street and, without looking to see who it was, I quickly darted back into our house and locked the door behind me.

The voices got closer and closer until they were just outside the door. They were laughing, high voices; they didn't sound like Mum or Tiber. Then, gradually, they got quieter and further away, until there was no sound left but the steady thumps of music from next door. I ventured outside again.

I saw it immediately. There was something lodged in the gap between the lamppost and the bin where, only minutes before, there had been nothing. I looked up and down the street. The old man couldn't have been far away.

It had been bundled into a plastic bag so that it stayed in the space, but it came away easily when I tugged it.

Inside I found shiny, caramel-coloured acorns; there were five of them. I'd seen them on the table in Ms Doyle's room and she had told me what they were. These ones, though, were much bigger.

'Do you know what an oak tree looks like, Leelu?' Ms Doyle had asked me.

I shook my head.

She grabbed one of her tree books and licked her finger to flick through the pages. 'Here . . .' She prodded one of the pictures to show a huge tree: its trunk was staggeringly thick and its branches bent at angles, making wiggly lines.

'One little acorn,' Ms Doyle said, 'and it grows into this. Amazing, right?'

I nodded; it truly did not seem possible.

It made me think of the towering shea tree that grew near my grandmother's house. She'd died a few years ago, but I still remembered visiting her. She was an ancient-looking woman, but when she smiled, she looked as young as a girl.

'Magic!' she used to tell me, grasping my hand with hers. 'Magic can appear in the most unexpected places, Leelu. It's just about looking out for it.'

I held the acorns in my hand and thought about the five trees they could grow into. I imagined them starting to sprout in my hand; I would have to throw them into the road. Their roots would shoot downwards and split the tarmac while their branches reached upwards, up to the sky, growing taller with each second that passed.

They would tower over my house, those five trees, and you would no longer be able to see the buildings all around. It would be a little island of trees; an island of my own.

I knocked at the old man's door again, but there was still no answer. I pressed my ear to it, and I was sure I heard someone moving inside, but when I knocked once more, the door remained resolutely shut. I rotated the acorns in my hand and then took the smallest one, holding it tightly in my fist so you couldn't see that it was there.

I squeezed hard, and wished.

Let the door open.

Open, open, open.

For a moment nothing happened.

Then I heard the sound of the lock clicking.

The door slowly edged open.

25

There were the piles and piles of things lining the walls in every direction, though there was no sign of the old man.

'Hello?' I called down the corridor, but my voice sounded little, as though it had been absorbed by all the things and couldn't get through.

But then, in answer, there was a large crash from the sitting room. Dog began to bark.

As I opened the door, he rushed up to me, sniffed my hand and then bounded back to the old man, who was lying on the floor, unmoving. Dog rushed back and forth between us as though trying to tell me, *This way, this way*.

I knelt down next to the old man.

His eyes were closed and he lay ever so still, as though he was sleeping, only without the snoring.

'Are you all right? Can you hear me?' I said.

There was the smallest flicker of movement beneath the old man's eyelids. A twitch.

'I'll get help,' I said. 'Try not to move.'

I started to stand up, but just then the man's eyes flew open and he spoke.

'No help,' he said. 'No help. It can't be helped, it really can't.'

'But are you all right?' I asked. 'Can you get up?'

The old man took a deep breath and tried to move, but he winced with pain and stopped straight away.

'I don't suppose you could give me one of those acorns, could you?' he asked, pointing to my bulging pocket.

I passed him one of the bigger ones.

He held it tightly, whispering to himself, and after that he was able to roll onto his side and stand up.

He stretched his arms out wide, making the branches hanging from the ceiling beside him dance.

'That's betterer,' he said.

'The acorn fixed you . . .' I said.

'It stopped the pain. For a titbit.'

'But how does it . . . How do the things do that? I've been able to—'

'Make things happen?' the old man said, smiling to himself a little.

'Yes.'

'You needed things to happen, and so they happened.'

'But . . .' The room felt like it was spinning, rotating on an axis, turning upside down.

'You were the one who found the things because you needed them. Head, shoulders—'

'Needs and toes,' I finished for him.

'Well, yes,' said the old man. 'It really is that simple.'

And then he started rummaging through his things, as he had done the first time I was there.

'What are you looking for?' I asked him, but he ignored the question and instead passed me a shoebox from one of the piles.

It was stuffed with conkers and leaves and feathers and twigs, all jumbled up together. I wasn't sure what it was he wanted me to do, but I started to look through the box and divide the things inside into piles, as I'd seen him do, covering the floor with even more stuff.

I paused over one of the conkers. It looked a bit different from the others, although I couldn't say exactly why that was. It was roughly the same size, colour and shape but there was something that marked it out as unlike the rest. I turned it over in my fingers, examining it for a moment.

It almost seemed to glow, although it wasn't glowing, of course. But it *felt* as though it was glowing.

'Yes, that's one,' said the old man, and he plucked the conker from my hand.

'One what?'

'A wonder. One that will work,' he replied. He placed the conker in one of the glass jars and then tucked the jar behind some other boxes, out of sight.

I carried on looking through the box the old man had given me. Again, for a reason I couldn't explain, I stopped to examine one of the feathers. It didn't have any particular markings but there was something about it that marked it as different. Like the conker, it seemed to give off its own light, in a way that I couldn't exactly see, though I could feel it.

'And another!' cried the old man, and he whisked the feather from me, squirrelling it away. 'You've got an ear for this!'

'Those are the ones that have power. The magic ones,' I said finally when the old man had taken another feather I'd been lingering over.

'The wonders,' he corrected me.

'But how do I see it? How do I know that?'

'How many times do I have to tell you? Because you need it,' he said. 'You need it, and so it needs you. The magic wants to be wanted and used. It calls out to you because it knows you'll use it.'

'And you need it too?' I asked.

'I think that's fairly oblivious,' said the old man. Suddenly he looked very small among all the things that surrounded him.

'I am trying,' he went on, 'to do something quite splentacular . . .' All of a sudden he stopped talking and, sniffing something in the air, turned to a corner of the room and started burrowing amidst the boxes to retrieve something.

'What are you trying to do?' I asked.

The old man didn't bother answering but I didn't ask again. I had realized by now that he would answer me eventually, if I waited.

It was when he was lining up a bundle of twigs that the reply came.

He looked right at me with his brown, bright eyes as though seeing me for the very first time.

'I am trying to fly,' he told me.

26

Mum had started to shout.

I sat in our bedroom with my hands tightly covering my ears, but I could still hear everything she was saying. She'd found Tiber in the chicken shop we'd gone to together and marched him back to the house, holding his arm so tightly that it seemed she would never let go.

I'd got back before they had, only just in time to see them walking down the street, Mum half dragging Tiber alongside her.

'. . . and your sister!' she was shrieking now. 'How do you think this will look to her?'

I heard Tiber mumble something, and though I couldn't hear what exactly, I could tell that it made Mum very angry. Her voice rose and she spat out her words in shrieks.

'You do not . . . you do not speak like that,' she shouted. Every loud word hit me like a brick. I tried to block out the sound by holding my pillow over my ears but it didn't seem to make any difference. All the magic I had felt at the old man's house seemed to leak away. Nothing glowed; everything looked dull, grey.

If Betsy and her family were back, they would have heard it all. They would be the ones calling *us* the Noisy Neighbours. I wished I could tell Mum and Tiber what I was thinking; it might make Mum stop shouting for a moment; it might even make them smile. But the shouting continued.

'I will not accept this . . . this . . . this behaviour!' she yelled.

I wondered if the old man could hear her. Dog was probably looking up, his eyes searching worriedly for the source of the angry voices. I decided that they probably wouldn't be able to hear because of all the things piled up against the walls. They would block out the sound, stop it from getting through.

I hoped they would.

'Get up to your room,' Mum shouted. 'And stay there!'

Tiber came bursting through the door, as strong as a wind, and slammed it behind him. One of its hinges gave way so it didn't shut properly and hung crookedly.

'Stupid!' he yelled. I don't know who he was talking about. Mum. The door. Himself.

He threw himself down on his bed, falling like a stone. It creaked and strained with the weight and I wondered if it would break too. Tiber lay so still, face down, that I wondered how he could breathe properly.

But Tiber was not one for staying still, and a moment later he was up again, pacing the room as though it was a cage and he a lion.

'Are you all right?' I asked him.

He looked over as though he had only just noticed I was there.

'I'm just . . . I'm just . . .' Tiber said, but he was shaking as he spoke, too angry to find the right words. Then he started speaking so fast I didn't think he would ever stop.

'They didn't ask us, did they? Didn't ask us if we wanted to come here, did they? Didn't ask us if we wanted to leave Dad behind. We wouldn't have left him, Leelu, would we? If we'd been given the choice, we wouldn't have gone without him, would we? You miss him as much as I do, don't you? I see you looking out at the sky every night. You're looking for the moon, aren't you? Because Dad told you that stupid thing about being together on the moon. But none of it's true. He's not really with you when you look at the moon. He's far away, he's back at home. Where *we* should be.'

'Stop it,' I said. 'Stop it.' I wished I could block out his shouting, like I'd wished to block out Mum's before.

Just then, Mum came into the bedroom. She looked at me, seeing the tears that had started to build in my eyes.

'Don't you go upsetting Leelu now,' she told Tiber, and pulled me out of bed and out of the room.

She tried to shut the door behind us, but because of the hinge it still wouldn't close properly and got stuck on the carpet.

'It's OK, Leelu,' Mum said to me when we were downstairs. She brought both hands up to her face for a moment, as though hiding from me or unable to look at me. I thought she might start to cry. But then she brought her hands down again and stared hard at the wall. 'It'll be OK,' she said in the end.

She made me a drink of squash and found some digestives in the cupboard, which I ate because I didn't know what to say. Mum ate one too, and then there was just the sound of us crunching the powdery, dust-like biscuits.

I drank my squash, although Mum had put too much syrup in and it tasted very sweet. 'Do you feel better?' she asked me after we had eaten two biscuits each.

I looked at her over the rim of my glass and nodded ever so slightly.

I sipped at the too-sweet drink and I didn't tell her what I was really thinking.

I didn't tell her that she'd been shouting just as loudly as Tiber.

I didn't tell her that it wasn't Tiber who had upset me.

I didn't tell her that it was because what he'd said was true.

If anyone had asked us, we would not have left Dad behind.

27

The next night, almost as soon as Mum had gone to work, Tiber took the keys and went to open the front door.

'Where are you going?' I asked him.

'I've got to get out, Leelu,' he said. 'I feel trapped in here. I'll make sure I'm back before she is. She'll never know. You won't say anything, will you?'

All day, Mum and Tiber hadn't spoken to each other properly. They'd fall silent if the other came into the room; they wouldn't even look at one another. It was as though they didn't even exist for each other any more. There was a thick silence, a tension strung across the air, before they started talking to me in overloud voices about nothing important.

'Just make sure you're back before she is,' I said. 'And be careful' – remembering why Mum had shouted the night before. Part of me didn't want Tiber to leave, but then, with him out, I could go and see the old man again, unnoticed too. I wanted to go. Partly because I hadn't asked all the questions I had for him, but also because he still needed help. I remembered the rotting smells in the kitchen, the encrusted plates piled up. No one ever visited him. I wondered if he was lonely sitting in his funny sitting room with all those things he had collected for company.

As soon as Tiber had disappeared down the street, hands in pockets, head down as though he was worried that Mum might jump out at him, I left too. I'd found a way to stop the door from locking when I closed it by twisting a little button. I tested it out a few times to make sure that it worked and then slipped across to the old man's front door.

'Hello,' I called through the letter box. 'It's me; it's Leelu.' I didn't even know his name and I had never told him mine, but surely he'd recognize my voice.

I could see Dog running up and down the hallway. He pressed his wet nose to my fingers, which were peeking through the letter box. Saying hello.

Behind him the old man was walking towards the door.

'Come in, come in,' he said, a little impatiently, when he opened it. He hurried back to the sitting room, with Dog following, tail held high.

The room seemed even more chaotic than before. There were so many piles on the floor that there was hardly anywhere to stand. I tiptoed round the edge and perched on a little stool that I spotted amidst the piles.

'I'm trying something; I'm trying sums and things,' the old man said.

'You're trying to fly?' I asked.

'Well, yes, that's the wonder. And this might be the right mix of stuff. This could be it. Do you want to stay?' he said. 'It might not work.'

'Yes,' I said, and then, 'Don't worry if it doesn't work. One of my teachers at school says that mistakes are magic. They help you learn.'

Ms Doyle was always saying that, and though at first I hadn't understood what she meant, now I was getting the hang of it. If I got something wrong, Ms Doyle and I would work out what it was I didn't understand, and that helped me to remember the right way for the next time.

'OK,' said the old man. 'Here we go.'

He gathered the neat piles of things – sticks covered in light green fuzz, moss, dried-out leaves, pine cones, walnuts – into one big mess, and then, kneeling down because there was so much of it, he brought his arms around it all and started whispering.

He spoke so quietly that I couldn't make out what he was saying. They were disjointed half-words that I could not decipher.

The mass of things twitched, vibrated, and then, like the ball of moss on the night of the storm, it started to shake more violently.

The old man struggled to keep his arms around it. He held on to it desperately as though it was struggling in his embrace like a squirming creature that was trying to escape. Then a look came over him in a wave, one of total tranquillity, and his whole face relaxed.

It didn't seem like anything was happening, but when I looked at his feet, I saw, in between them and the floor, the smallest of gaps. He was floating above the carpet, just by a whisker. If I hadn't looked closely, I wouldn't have seen it.

I looked away and then back again, unable to believe that what I was seeing was true.

Then, like a helium balloon released into the air, the old man began to float upwards.

Not just a little: he rose further and further off the floor.

He rose past my nose so I had to tilt my head upwards to look at him, then further still.

Up, up he went as he held the mass of things in his hands.

He laughed as he rose. It made me think of Dad laughing like it couldn't be contained; laughter that made you feel brighter.

I heard myself laughing out loud too, just like Dad, astonished and bewildered and amazed. I was light with excitement, as though I too was rising upwards like a stream of bubbles that played in the air.

When he had almost reached the ceiling, the old man let go of the bundle of stuff, and then, very suddenly, he dropped to the floor with a loud thud, disturbing a pile of boxes and causing a tower of jars to topple and crash around him.

It was the same crashing sound I'd heard the previous evening.

I ran to his side once more. 'Are you all right?' I said urgently. 'Can you hear me?'

He was muttering something, and I had to bring my ear close to the floor to hear what he was saying.

'Did you see me?' he asked. 'Did you see me fly?'

'Yes, I did,' I said. 'You did it! You flew. For a little bit anyway.'

'I just can't make it last for a song. There's something up with the mix of wonders. I'm missing something.'

'Are you hurt? Can you get up?'

'I'm all right,' he said a little impatiently, but he looked very white.

'Maybe you shouldn't try to fly again unless I'm here to help. In case you hurt yourself.'

'Maybe,' the old man said. 'Maybe.'

'What do you think you are missing from the mix? Do you want me to help you find it?' I asked.

He didn't answer at first but looked like he was thinking hard about something. Then he said, 'Yes, please. I'm not sure I'm going to be able to find it on my ownsome. And then it might be too late. Tick-tock, tick-tock.'

'OK . . .' I hesitated over what to call him. 'What's your name? I'm called Leelu.'

'Leelu,' he said as though he had always known what I was called. 'My name's the same as it was before.'

'What was it before, then?'

'Bo,' he said. 'My name's Bo.'

28

'What's going on, little fish?'

Betsy was at our front door, looking even browner than she had before.

It had been two weeks since we'd seen each other, and suddenly there seemed too much to tell her, too much that had happened while she was away. And not all of it was good. I felt my voice catch in my throat, and for a moment I thought I might start to cry.

'Come on, let's play,' Betsy said, taking in my face. 'No problem made worse by football. Apart from broken leg. Do you have broken leg?'

I smiled and shook my head.

'Come on then!' she said. 'We have to keep warm in this grey, cold place. It's so cold here after Colombia! But we can bring the warmth ourselves, hey?'

Betsy wanted us to practise dribbling and passing the ball to one another, and Mum said we could play in the small concrete park just across the road from our house as long as we stayed where she could see us.

'We have to kick right to each other,' Betsy insisted. 'So the person does not have to move even a little bit.'

I was terrible at first, but after a while we became quite good at kicking the ball straight to each other so that we did not have to move even a little bit. When Betsy was satisfied that we were doing it well enough, we stopped. She brought out some cake that she had brought back from Colombia and wanted me to try.

I dusted the sweet crumbs from my mouth and told her everything that had happened.

I told her about Tiber disappearing on the night of the storm; how he and Mum were fighting all the time; and also, of course, about Bo.

Betsy's eyes bulged when I told her about him stopping the storm and flying in his overcrowded little sitting room.

'But someone cannot fly. Aeroplanes fly. And birds. And superheroes. It's not real, someone flying?' She cocked her head to the side.

'I'm telling you, Betsy. It really did happen.' My voice came out louder than I'd meant. 'He was using the wonders to do it. Just like I used them to make things happen. But flying is much harder: you have to have the right mix of wonders. He just floated up off the ground; he flew!'

'OK, OK, little fish. I don't not believe you; it's just that I never see this before. But if you say it's true, I know it's true.'

'It is true,' I said. 'I know it sounds like it can't be real but I saw it happen, I swear to you.'

'I believe. I believe you.' Betsy suddenly reached out for my hand and squeezed it tightly.

'Can I meet Bo?' she said. 'I want to have the power too. I could use against my brothers when they gang up on me.'

I told her that I would go and see him once Mum had left for work, after Tiber had gone out with his friends.

'I come tonight,' she said. 'My father is at work. My grandma will not notice if I am careful.'

We passed the ball to one another a couple more times, but at first Betsy kept missing the ball. Once we were in the swing of it, though, we sent the ball right to each other's feet – and then we went our separate ways, arranging to meet up later that evening. Betsy was going to listen out for our door slamming twice – once for Mum leaving and a second time for Tiber – and then come round so we could go and see Bo.

*

157

It was very cold that night. I wished I was wearing something warmer as we knocked gently on Bo's front door.

I heard the heavy tread of Dog coming along the hall and knew that Bo would not be far behind.

'This is Betsy,' I told him when he opened the door. 'She's come to help as well.' He did not seem surprised to see her with me.

'Hello, Mr Bo,' Betsy said.

'I'm not sure if it's going to work tonight,' Bo said as though we had asked him a question. 'It doesn't feel quite right. I'm forgetting something, but I can't remember what it is I'm forgetting.'

'Don't worry. We'll help,' I said.

'Yes, we help,' Betsy echoed.

Bo directed us to one of the upstairs rooms to find more wonders that could still be used. The rooms were small but were made smaller still because every wall was lined with boxes right up to the ceiling.

'My, Mr Bo,' Betsy said. 'Where does he get all this stuff?'

'I'm not sure.'

We started looking at boxes and sifting through their contents. I quickly found a walnut that I knew would work, but Betsy was having trouble.

'I don't know what I look for,' she said.

I tried to explain about the glow, but then I saw her discarding a pine cone that I saw very clearly would work, and realized that she just couldn't see it.

'Come on,' I said. 'Let's go back downstairs. Let's see if Bo will let us use some of these things.'

As before, he had made piles on the floor. He was counting them and then turning a thing over in his hands, carefully inspecting it.

'Bo? Bo?' I said. 'Can we show Betsy how to use the things? She's not seen it before.'

'It's still not quite right,' he said. 'I don't think I'll fly tonight. You can use the wonders I'm not using.' He gestured to a small pile of things he'd put to one side. 'You won't be able to do all that much. They're not that powerful. They come from a bit away from the middle of the place. A little to the left of the right.'

'So some wonders hold more power than others?' I asked, ignoring Bo's riddles.

'Of course, a horse,' he said. 'That's why I have to use certain things to make me fly, but this little acorn, well, this could take those feathers for a spin.'

'Show us, Mr Bo,' Betsy said. 'Show us the feather spin.'

'All right,' he said. He took the acorn in his hand and whispered to himself. This time, of course, we didn't see it twitch in his fist, but I thought I could tell when it did because his expression changed a little.

All of a sudden the pile of feathers flew into the air like they were the flock of birds they had come from.

They flew upwards, one after the other, perfectly synchronized, and then fanned out around Betsy and me so we were surrounded by darting blurs of white and grey and black. Then they fell around us, gently resting the end of each tip upon another to make a circle of feathers on the floor.

'Wow! Mr Bo!' Betsy squealed delightedly. 'That was something!'

'That was nothing, nothing,' Bo said, puffing out his chest a bit as though he was secretly pleased.

'Leelu, why don't *you* do something?' He passed me another acorn.

I suddenly felt nervous. I held the acorn carefully in my fist and then thought with all my might. Feeling the little twist of movement, I opened my eyes to see the piles of leaves whipping around and around on themselves in fury. Like a tornado that spun and spun. The spiral of leaves travelled across the room and around each of us, before stacking themselves on top of one another in a teetering, fragile pile in Betsy's open hand.

'Leelu! That's amazing!' she cried out.

'That was quite beautiful,' Bo added.

And I – I couldn't stop smiling.

29

Much to her annoyance, Betsy couldn't make the things do anything for her.

Bo said simply that she didn't need to – that was why it didn't happen – although it didn't stop Betsy from trying. Every time we went to Bo's house she spent some portion of the evening holding the last acorn, fist clenched and eyes closed, her cheeks flushed red, trying to make something fly.

The weather became colder and colder.

The season was changing.

As though affected by the weather, Mum seemed greyer too. Like the overcast sky, promising nothing more than a cold wind. She and Tiber spoke a little more now – they'd stopped ignoring each other completely – but there was still a distance between them. Each time they talked Mum's face became pinched and drained of colour, much like the trees outside, which had shed their leaves, their bare branches growing in sharp angles.

Whenever I was outside I had to be wrapped up in jumpers, coats, scarves and gloves; it was difficult to move, being so bundled up. But nothing seemed to keep the cold from whistling down my neck and settling in my bones. The feeling of stiffness, of tightness, stayed with me, and I ached even more for the warmth of home, where the sun's rays beat down upon you, urging you to relax, to open up, to slow in its fierce heat.

It was such a long time since we'd seen Dad.

It was the end of summer when we'd first arrived here, but now the days were darker, colder; I couldn't ignore how long it had been. Despite Mum and Dad's protests that he would come soon, months had passed, and still no one knew when it would be.

'Stop asking me about your father!' Mum had exploded one day when I questioned her.

She stepped away from me and put her hands on the kitchen sink, letting her head drop. She looked like she was trembling. A moment later she turned back to me.

'I'm sorry – I didn't mean to shout. But there's nothing I can do about it.'

'I just wish he was here,' I said.

'I know,' Mum said. 'I know. I miss him too.'

There was so much more I wanted to say. I wanted to ask why we had come without him. Why it was taking so long. What was it that Mum could do nothing about? But I didn't want her to yell again. She was like that so often these days. Silent, grey and unspeaking, and then shouting at the top of her voice as if everything was always boiling away just under the surface. Ready, at any moment, to spill over.

Although I still missed Dad as much as I had when we first arrived, I realized I didn't have as much time to miss him as I once did. Tiber said we were getting used to him not being there and that it wasn't a good thing. Mum would get upset when she heard Tiber saying that, and Tiber would cock his head to one side and reply, 'But it's the truth, isn't it?'

Ms Doyle told me that I was doing really well, and though I felt I was improving when I was with her, every time I returned to my class I wasn't so sure.

Mrs Winters was making us practise for the tests we had to take at the end of the year. We had to sit in silence when we did them. Whenever we did the practice tests everyone else seemed very busy writing. They scribbled knowingly, and I came to hate the sound of their pencils scratching away.

It was the sound of everyone knowing what to do, while I felt clueless; I just didn't understand.

I was getting better though. My marks began to improve, slowly at first, and then one day we were taking a test and I realized that I hadn't been listening to the others writing; I'd been too busy working on my answers. After that, the dread I felt at the work lessened, although I still felt shy around my classmates. I didn't know how I could possibly start talking to them after I'd been so quiet all this time.

It was different when I was at Bo's with Betsy. Bo was excited by all the wonders I'd been able to find, and Betsy was even trying to teach him to play football.

'No magic!' she demanded when Bo used one of the walnuts to make the football jump from his foot and dance across the ceiling. It wasn't the best place to play football because there was so much stuff around, but it was good that Betsy could show us something that she was good at while we were able to show her our powers.

Every time Tiber left the house I would go over to Bo's. When her father was working nights, Betsy would come too. I tried not to think how angry Mum would be if she knew that I was sneaking out. I told myself that she would not know anything was different.

Tiber went out most evenings. I never saw him come back, and I still had no idea what he was doing on those long, cold nights. One morning, though, I saw him playing around with the phone – but when he noticed me, he sat up and quickly stuffed it under his pillow. He made a great show of picking at one of the stickers that had been welded to the headboard of his bed by a previous owner. He had a detached look on his face that reminded me of the hard concrete buildings that surrounded us. I pretended not to notice anything and delivered the message from Mum that breakfast was ready.

I sneaked back when we were all eating, pretending I needed to go to the toilet, and discovered what it was he was hiding from me. He had a brand-new phone, black, shiny, impossibly thin. It was light and cool in my hands. I covered the sleek screen with my fingerprints, which I tried to wipe off with my sleeve. I knew it was expensive – I couldn't understand how Tiber could possibly have paid for it. I stuck it back under his pillow, but when I looked for it later, it had gone. I didn't see it again, and though part of me wanted to forget that I had ever seen it, another part couldn't leave it alone. How had Tiber got hold of a phone like that? And where had it gone now?

After I had found the phone I thought Tiber looked a bit different. There was something about him that had changed, but I couldn't quite put my finger on it.

Mum had taken on more shifts and worked every night now, even over the weekend. When I got to see her, she was so tired after being up all night that I sometimes felt like she was a different person.

She was slower at doing things, more tearful. She would get upset over little accidents, like when she knocked over a mug and it smashed on the floor. When I spoke to her, it was like she couldn't hear me properly or wasn't really listening. It made me feel a bit like I had at school; like there was glass or an invisible line between us.

I felt more like myself when I was with Bo and Betsy.

'Now, the walnuts,' Bo said to us one evening. It was almost dark by the time I got back from school now. Bo always lit lots and lots of candles instead of using electric lights, and we sat bathed in their warm glow. 'The walnuts are from right in the middle. The very, very centre.'

He talked like this a lot and we didn't really understand what he meant. Betsy and I looked at each other, confused.

'What do you mean?' I asked. 'The middle of what?'

'Of the place,' he said.

'What place?'

'The one I've been telling you all about.' Bo laughed. The sound was light, tinkling like a bell.

We had been going round like this in circles for days.

'Where do you mean?' Betsy asked.

'The place, the place.' His eyes twinkled.

'That's where you got the things from?' I asked.

Bo nodded. 'The things come from the place. They slip between the crackles and the holes. I collect up everything I can and try to work out what is a wonder and what is not.'

'Where is this place, Mr Bo?' Betsy asked again.

'It can be close. But it can be far. Depending on where you are, of course,' he said.

Betsy and I both sighed in frustration. Sometimes, just as Bo seemed about to tell us something, he would veer off in another direction where we couldn't follow.

Bo revealed things about the place that made it seem impossible that it could be real.

He told us that the trees could move; that they used their branches like arms and could pick you up so you were far, far off the ground. High above everything else.

He told us that there were little lights floating in the air around you like dandelion seeds. They followed you about, and the more you walked, the more you collected, so you could always find the path you'd taken by the trail of lights behind you. I imagined the lights zigzagging and looping, making a whirling, dazzling scribble.

He spoke of a great walnut tree that was at the centre of it all. The most powerful things came from close to the walnut tree, and the further you got from it, the less powerful things were.

The place was full of birds, although you could only rarely see them because they were incredibly shy and hid among the trees, out of sight. Bo had only ever seen one there, but he had collected their feathers of course.

Bo had taught me how to look at the things he had collected; I could tell which were more powerful by the way they glowed. It was to do with the brightness of the glow, the feel of its shine.

We were getting ready for Bo to try to fly again. He wanted to find a place outside – he thought being closer to trees and nature would help, so on some nights we went out with Dog to try and find the perfect spot.

'Why do you want to fly, Mr Bo?' Betsy asked one day after we'd looked at some trees planted in a circle which Bo had dismissed because they were too close to the houses. Looking at the buildings that surrounded us, I wondered if we would ever find the right place; I always felt overlooked, wherever we were in this city.

'Because I want to go home, of course, a horse,' Bo answered.

'Where do you come from, Bo? Where's home?' I asked.

'I come from a long way away, a journey and a day.'

'Like us!' Betsy exclaimed.

'I suppose. But you know the way back to your place, don't you?'

Betsy giggled. 'Well, our parents know. But maybe, Mr Bo, there is a more simple way. I go back home to my country on an aeroplane.'

'There's no way other than the way I came. At least, I don't think there is. I left it a long time ago, and I've been trying to fly home ever since. But I definitely didn't come by aeroplane,' Bo replied. 'Flying is the only way I can get my bones home. And Dog's too – don't forget about Dog.'

Betsy reached down to rub one of Dog's ears; she looked as though she was pondering something.

'Will Dog fly too?' I asked.

'Of course, a horse,' Bo said. 'I certainly can't carry him all that way back.' He made a humphing sort of sound. 'I'd never get home.'

'Well, Mr Bo,' Betsy said. 'We have to get you both flying then.'

30

'Leelu, Leelu, wake up,' Mum said to me urgently.
'Have you seen your brother?'

I shook myself awake and looked over at
Tiber's bed. His duvet was still neatly pulled up.
He had not slept there. Mum's eyes were wide with
panic.

'Mum? You're back?'

'They sent me home, said I had the flu. But
forget about that. Tiber – where is he? When did
you last see him?'

'He's gone out,' I said. I knew there was no
point lying now.

'What do you mean, gone out?'

'He . . . He sometimes goes out when you go
to work. He always comes back.'

'Where does he go? Wait – you knew about
this?' Mum's voice rose.

'I'm sorry, Mum,' I said. 'I just . . . I couldn't

stop him. And he always comes back. He's there when I wake up.'

Mum exhaled heavily. 'I don't believe this,' she said. 'I'm calling the police.'

'He'll come back, Mum,' I said again. I wiped my eyes properly to wake myself up. 'He'll be here really soon. He always comes back.'

'How long? How long has this been going on?'

'Erm, for a little while. Since you started working nights, I suppose.'

'So from the very beginning then. What time? What time does he come home?'

'I don't know. I'm always asleep.'

'OK, fine,' Mum said. She sounded dangerously calm. 'Go back to sleep.'

'What are you going to do?'

'I am going to wait for him to come home,' she said. She sneezed violently five times without stopping, and I remembered that she had come back from work because she wasn't well.

'Are you OK?' I asked her, but she didn't answer and left the room. I could hear the anger in every footstep as she stamped down the stairs. *Don't be cross with me*, I wanted to shout. *Tiber is the one who went out.*

But I knew that I was not being truthful, not even to myself. I dreaded to think what would happen if Mum found out that I went to see Bo every night when Tiber left the house. Even though I was perfectly safe, I knew that Mum wouldn't like it and would stop me from going.

I was fully awake now. Outside it was as dark as it could get, with the orange streetlights that never went out. I had the feeling that it was still a long time until morning.

It looked chilly on the street, the trees bare for winter. I wondered, as I imagined Mum did, where Tiber would go on such a cold, dark night.

He had always been an adventurer. Dad used to tell us that as soon as Tiber could walk he would go exploring.

'He's just worked out what his legs are for,' he would say. 'I turned my back for maybe a minute and he was gone. I couldn't find him anywhere. You know where he was? Outside, down the garden.'

Tiber would let Dad ruffle his hair but he'd mock-complain, 'Not the hair! Not the hair!' though I think he liked Dad doing it and telling that story. It was about who Tiber was.

I slipped out of bed. It was chilly, so I pulled on a pair of socks and my school jumper, which was lying on the floor. I tiptoed out of the bedroom and looked down the stairs. There were no lights on. Mum must have been sitting in the dark.

I sat on the top step of the narrow staircase and hugged my arms around me to keep warm. Part of me wanted to go down to Mum, to climb onto her lap like Tiber and I used to, but I knew that, even if she hadn't been so angry with me, I was too big now; I wouldn't fit.

We waited there in the darkness, me and Mum, for what felt like hours and hours. Maybe it was because it was cold and the lights weren't on that it felt so long. Time stretched out in front of me like a black pool; it had no end, no edges.

Finally I heard Tiber's key scratching at the lock and heard his light tread on the carpet. He closed the door softly and started to climb the stairs, stretching out his legs so he could take three steps at a time.

He saw me sitting at the top, but just as he started to say my name, Mum spoke.

Her voice cut through everything.

'Why bother going to bed?' she said.

'Mum,' Tiber stammered.

'Yes? You have something else to say to me?'

'I . . . I . . . always come home.'

'Home? This isn't a home to you. You don't treat it like one. Why bother coming back at all?'

'Maybe I shouldn't,' Tiber said, although his voice trembled a little. I could see him staring at Mum, frozen where he was when she first spoke, halfway up the stairs. Then something seemed to release inside him, like the air escaping from a balloon, and he turned and sat on the steps. Crumpled, defeated.

'Where have you been?' Mum said quietly.

'Just out.'

'Out? Where is that? What do you mean, Tiber? Out? Tell me the truth.'

'I meet up with friends,' Tiber said. 'Friends from school.'

'At this time of night? What are you doing with these so-called friends?'

'You know, just stuff.'

'No, I don't know,' Mum said. 'I don't know you any more. My Tiber would not do this to me, to Leelu. You were meant to be looking after your little sister. What if she needed you? What if she went out looking for you?'

I held my breath. I wondered if Tiber would tell Mum about the night of the storm when he'd found me outside.

He hung his head. 'I'm sorry,' he said.

This was the bit where Mum would say she was sorry too. She would say she was sorry that she'd

176

moved us here, that we'd had to leave Dad behind, that she hadn't been here because she was always at work. But that was not what she said.

'I am disgusted by your behaviour.'

Tiber snapped. 'Disgusted by my behaviour. What about *your* behaviour? You never knew I wasn't here because *you* weren't here.'

'That's neither here nor there,' Mum said. 'It's the only job I could get . . .'

Back home Mum used to work in a law office. She wasn't one of the lawyers, but Dad said that without her the whole place would fall apart and that she could have been a lawyer if she wanted to. Whenever he said this, Mum would sigh as though she wanted him to change the subject, and when I asked her why, she would say something that didn't seem to answer the question.

'Sometimes you have to start looking forwards, not back,' Mum would say, in a final sort of way that I knew meant she thought there was nothing more to say on the matter.

Now, in the face of Tiber's rage, which seemed to shoot around the room, knocking against the walls, ricocheting off corners, Mum continued to plead: 'If I could find something that didn't mean I had to be out every night, I would have taken it. I would be here if I could.'

As she spoke, tears started to spring from Mum's eyes, but Tiber was exploding with anger now. I imagined it like the fireworks I had seen bursting in the sky in every direction on bonfire night. They had come one after the other, like gunshots, filling the air with their colour and their noise.

I had been at Bo's house, and we had hugged Dog to comfort him. He trembled at the sound; his whole body a shaking mass of grey.

'You left Dad behind,' Tiber shouted. 'You made *us* leave him.'

'It was for the bes—'

'No! No!' he screamed. 'It's not – it's not for the best. It's for the *worst*. We should never have come here. But we are here now, and *I* . . . *I'm* making the best I can of it.'

With that, he ran out of the house.

'Tiber! Tiber! Come back, come home!' Mum shouted and shouted.

Over and over.

He didn't come back.

31

Mum picked me up from school the day after Tiber left and pretended that everything was normal. But she jumped at every sound and kept looking around as we walked. Later, I realized she was looking out for Tiber.

Her flu had got worse. Her eyes and nose were red, and she sneezed in a way that made her whole body jolt and start.

'Where's Tiber?' I asked.

'I don't know, Leelu. I'm not sure. He went to school. But he wouldn't come home with me. He said he'd be back later, whatever that means.'

The house seemed very empty without him stretched across the sofa. I used to hate it when he did that because it didn't leave room for anyone else. But now, sitting there next to Mum, I wished he was there, taking up all the space.

'I'm staying home tonight,' Mum told me as she cooked dinner. She was making her special

179

jollof rice, and the smell should have made me feel better but my stomach turned over. I thought instead of Bo, and Betsy waiting to hear the door slams of Mum and Tiber leaving.

A veil of mystery surrounded Tiber now. The friends he spoke of seemed like dark, shadowy figures. I wondered, not for the first time, how he'd got hold of the expensive phone I'd found. Had he stolen it? But from where? Surely he didn't have the money to buy it. And I remembered how differently he acted now. How distant he was when he was with us, like he was somewhere else. His new friends had taken him away from us – or perhaps, I thought, it was just Tiber himself who had done that.

And I couldn't stop worrying about Mum. She was pretending that everything was normal when it felt like it was falling apart. I noticed that she kept having to stop cooking to hold her head in her hands.

'It's just a headache,' she reassured me as I hovered around her anxiously. 'It's a splitting one.'

I hated it when Mum said that about her headaches. Like the pain was so bad, her head was going to crack and break into two pieces.

Then we heard Tiber open the door.

He was there in front of us, and for a moment he smiled at me. Like everything was OK really. He was the same smiling joker. My big brother.

I ran over and threw my arms around him. I felt his close around me tightly for just a second. But when I released him, I could see that he had stopped smiling. He and Mum were staring at each other, their faces as blank and solid as a wall.

Finally Mum spoke. One word.

'Hungry?'

Tiber nodded.

Mum made up three plates. I was glad to hear the comforting kitchen sounds of the spoon scraping along the saucepan, the plates chiming against each other as she unstacked them. It was almost like things were normal again.

Then we all sat eating, balancing the plates on our knees. Tiber ate everything on his plate, but I could only manage some of mine and Mum didn't eat very much at all. Forkfuls of food almost made it to her mouth, and then it was like she had forgotten what she was doing and they ended up back on her plate again.

It was the quietest dinner I could remember us having. There were only the sounds of our chomping and chewing, forks knocking against plates and Mum's occasional sneezes and coughs.

'You not going to work?' Tiber said in the end, a scraped-clean plate in front of him.

'Not tonight,' Mum said. 'I'm here. I thought we could try and call Dad. See if we can get hold of him.'

'OK,' Tiber said.

But when we tried to ring him, it went straight to voicemail, so we left a rather strange message: we all went quiet and Mum just asked him to call us back and then Tiber said that we missed him. Before I was able to say anything, the message time had run out.

It seemed like the only way Mum and Tiber could get along was if they didn't speak to each other much. The next night Mum didn't say anything as, still off work, she watched him leave the house to see his friends. And Tiber didn't make any comment when Mum said that she was going back to work because she was feeling better.

Mum was worried about leaving me, now she knew that Tiber went out and that I would be on my own. I had to look away when she told me not to answer the door, wrote down her number at work for emergencies and asked me again and again if I was sure I didn't mind.

'We really need the money,' Mum said. 'Otherwise I'd never leave you alone, but . . .' She couldn't finish the sentence and left it dangling there. So I didn't have to lie to her about going round to see Bo with Betsy; I just looked the other way and Mum thought that I was upset with her.

'I'm sorry, Leelu. I don't know what else to say,' she said quietly, and then she left for work and closed the door behind her carefully so that it didn't slam as much as normal.

It was like it always was, except that no one was speaking to anyone else.

32

The next time I saw Bo it was just me; Betsy hadn't come round that night and I wondered if her dad had come back.

Bo didn't come to the door when I arrived. It had been left ajar for me. I closed it behind me and wondered how long it had been like that.

Some of the piles in the hallway had fallen over, so there wasn't room to walk past any more. I tucked them away as best I could, but they were teetering and fragile and looked like they might overbalance if you touched them.

I called out, 'I'm here, Bo. I'm just piling the things up – they've fallen down.'

'Hello, Leelu,' he said when I reached him. He was sitting a little stiffly in his armchair, his eyes unusually bright. Dog was pleased to see me; he stood up and walked round in circles for a bit and then sat down again. He did it three times in a row.

'Hi, Bo, how's it going?' I said, ruffling the sticky-up fur on Dog's head from side to side the way he likes. It was unusual not to see Bo springing around the house, rummaging and searching for things.

'Oh, you know. Sew and sew, needle and thread,' said Bo. 'Only . . . only . . .'

I looked at him.

He spoke very slowly. 'I had a bit of a stumble this morning.'

'Bo!' I cried out, and went to his side. 'Did you try to fly again?'

'I had to, Leelu,' he said, a bit gruffly. 'I know you said to wait for you and Betsy, but I was sure it was going to work. I even wrote you a note.'

There was a piece of paper with the message: *Gone flying. Gone home. Bo & Dog.* He'd done a drawing of himself flying through the sky.

'I'm sure I'll feel right as raindrops soon,' he said.

'Can't you use one of the wonders to help you?' I asked him anxiously.

'It only lasts for a little, piffly bit and I can't keep doing it,' he said. 'I'll be betterer soon, I know I will. It's just that I wasn't able to take Dog for his walk.' Dog looked up, his ears pricked. 'And you know how much he likes his walk. I wondered if you and Betsy might be able to take him out for a quick run-around. Not far – just to stretch his legs.'

It was night outside already, and though I would have done anything to help Bo, I couldn't help feeling frightened at the thought of walking the dark streets alone. Bo looked at me anxiously, his face even whiter than usual. Just then, he shifted creakily in his chair, and though he tried to stifle it, I heard him cry out in pain. He stared down at his legs in alarm, and then a look of tiredness, of defeat, came across his face. His expression crumpled in on itself like a dried-out, brown leaf that has become curly with age.

'Of course I will,' I said quickly. I thought, *I won't be on my own – I'll have Dog*. 'I'm not sure where Betsy is, but I can do it.'

'Thank you, Leelu,' said Bo. 'I told Dog that you would. Didn't I, Dog? I told you not to worry because Leelu would look after you.'

'I'll go now,' I said, before I could change my mind. 'Come on, Dog.'

Dog got up immediately and bounded towards the door. It was like he had fully understood everything Bo and I had just said.

We walked in the direction of the park. Dog didn't really need to wear a collar and lead, but Bo had told me that he had to have them because otherwise people were funny about it.

We stopped at a tree, a street corner and a lamppost that Dog liked the smell of. I tried to run a bit to give him more exercise, but I couldn't see round the corners in the darkness, so I slowed down.

The streets were narrow, and bent this way and that like a maze. We came out by a large block with lots of windows. Some were dark, some were lit up, but I felt like I was being watched through each one.

I was about to turn back when I glimpsed a group of people; one stood out among the others. It was something about the way they moved that stopped me. A tall, thin figure. Leaning forward in such a way that I knew for certain it was Tiber.

I stopped. I wanted to run up to him. I wanted to look into the eyes of his friends, but I couldn't see their faces because they were wearing hoods pulled up over their heads.

They were laughing about something. The sound seemed to jump towards me and hit me in the face. I realized that they were laughing at me.

'What is that, a wolf?'

'Walkies! Walkies!'

'Dog Girl!' one of them called out. 'What you staring at?'

They all began to shout that: '*Dog Girl, Dog Girl!*' in a chant.

Dog began to whine a bit and pulled gently on his lead to go back the way we'd come.

'Tiber,' I whispered. I watched him closely. He was still just a shape, but I was sure it was him.

'Hey, can I have your dog?' another of his friends shouted. 'We need a guard dog.'

There was more laughing. I strained my ears to hear Tiber's chuckle, so like Dad's, among the others.

'Yeah, let's take the dog,' said the one who'd first called me Dog Girl. 'We could train him up. To attack.'

I looked down at Dog. He was standing very still, his eyes fixed on them.

'Let's go, Dog,' I said, and we turned away.

'Where you going?'

'Dog Girl, come back.'

'Hey, come back.'

I heard footsteps behind me and turned to see that Tiber and his friends had started to follow us.

'Run, Dog, run!' I said.

My feet pounded the pavement. I heard them slapping down hard on the concrete. They sounded desperate, frantic. And beyond them I could hear the footsteps and shouts of the figures chasing us. They were getting louder; they were getting nearer.

My breath caught as I tried to run faster. Dog ran with an ease I did not possess. His stride lengthened, he accelerated, and I struggled to keep up with him.

I could feel his pull on the lead, and though I tried to keep hold of him, suddenly he was free.

'Dog!' I cried, but it came out as a gasp. He bounded lightly away from me, his lead trailing on the ground, and the shouts and jeers of the boys seemed to surround me.

I knew it would be only moments before they caught up with me.

I reached into my pocket. There was only one acorn left that wasn't used up. I rubbed it, and then clenched it tight.

Make me as fast as Dog. Let me outrun everyone.

It didn't feel like I was running any faster; if anything, I was putting in less effort now. My breath came easily and my feet flew across the ground, my stride lengthening and extending, as though my legs had grown.

The shouts got quieter and quieter; if I'd turned round, I knew I would have seen the boys far behind. They couldn't keep up with me. I had outrun them all.

But I didn't want to look back. I didn't want to see Tiber's face. As Dog charged on ahead of me, I kept running. Only when I got back to the corner leading to our street did I begin to slow down. Dog loped back to me. I picked up his lead limply, but then I collapsed onto him. He was solid beneath me, panting and warm.

He let me hold on to him, my fingers tangled in his fur. I felt weak now; slack and empty. Dog turned and looked up at me with those gentle, gentle eyes. He nudged me lightly. His nose felt wet and cold.

Come on, he seemed to be saying.

I stood up unsteadily, and started to walk. Together, side by side, we returned to Bo's house.

I closed the door behind us, pushing my weight against it until I heard the lock clicking into place.

I told myself that I wasn't hurt. It was true: there was not a mark on me. My legs throbbed slightly from sprinting, but other than that I was unchanged.

I told myself that I was safe now.

But I didn't believe it.

33

The next day it was the weekend and so we were all there together – Mum, Tiber and me – eating soup and toast for supper. Mum said she was too tired to cook anything else.

The toast was a bit overdone. Some of the corners were so brown they were almost black. It sounded loud, crunchy, as we took bites. None of us spoke much.

As I ate, I thought about the night before. I kept looking over my shoulder. I kept thinking there was someone there even when there wasn't. But I couldn't stop looking round, just in case.

'What's got into you?' Mum said, noticing.

'Nothing,' I said.

She shrugged and took a large bite of her toast; a piece fell off onto the floor.

I took a tiny peek at Tiber. He was staring straight ahead in a fixed sort of way, but then he saw me looking, and for a moment his eyes darted to meet mine. They seemed dark today; I couldn't read them. Then he looked down at the blackened crusts on his plate.

We hadn't spoken about it, but I was sure he was with the group of boys who'd chased Dog and me down the street. And I was sure he knew it was me. It was unspoken between us, like so many things.

As Tiber started stacking his pieces of burnt toast, there was a knock at the door. It was loud; it pounded. His hand faltered and his little pile of toast teetered and fell over. Mum gave a jump when she heard it. She looked from me to Tiber as though checking that it wasn't one of us rapping on the door.

Outside stood two police officers.

'Does a Tiber Olawale live here?' said one. She had short blonde hair and clear blue eyes that kept looking around.

'Yes,' said Mum.

'Are you . . .' The woman's radio crackled and I heard someone's voice at the other end. She turned a little dial on the radio and it faded. 'Sorry. Are you Tiber's mother?'

'Yes.'

'Can we come in, ma'am? We have a couple of questions for him.'

Mum stepped out of the way so that the police officers could come in. She glared furiously at Tiber.

'Leelu. Upstairs,' she said.

I obeyed, and quickly ran up the stairs towards my bedroom. But I didn't go in. I opened and shut the door so that Mum would think I was inside, but instead I waited out on the landing, listening to what was being said.

'What's this about?' Mum said. 'Is he in trouble?'

'We wanted to have a little chat about something that occurred last night,' said the other police officer. His voice was very deep. It did not sound friendly.

I wondered if the police had come because the boys had chased me. But then I realized that nobody knew about that apart from Dog and me. I hadn't even told Bo. I didn't want him to feel bad; after all, it had happened because he'd asked me to walk Dog.

Tiber didn't speak.

'Tiber? Come and sit down here,' the woman said. 'I'm Officer Rawley; this is Officer Peterson. We've just been talking to someone who says they saw you last night. Trip Matieson. Do you know who that is?'

'What's Trip been saying?' I heard Tiber say.

'What do you think he's been saying?' she said back, without missing a beat.

'I dunno,' Tiber said.

There was a silence where no one spoke.

Then I heard Mum. Her voice trembled. 'What's happened?'

I imagined her sitting there, squeezing her hands, clenching one and then the other, over and over. She always did that when she was nervous.

'Where were you last night, ma'am?' the policewoman asked.

'I was . . .' Mum hesitated; she paused. She didn't want to tell them the truth, I was sure of it. But then I imagined her saying to herself that it was no good lying. 'I was . . . I was at work. I work nights.'

'So you would not be able to confirm the whereabouts of your son at around eleven p.m. last night?'

'No,' Mum said quietly.

'Were you with Trip last night?' Officer Peterson asked. His voice filled our little house.

'I dunno,' Tiber said. 'Don't remember.'

'You can't remember what you did last night?' the policeman boomed. He was mocking Tiber; he sounded like he was about to start laughing.

'Can you tell us what happened last night?' Officer Rawley said. There was an urgency in her voice – I could hear it, cutting through everything else.

'Nothing happened.'

'Because Trip Matieson has made some pretty serious allegations about what you were doing last night. What you did . . . together,' the policeman said.

'He's lying,' Tiber said, and then, all in a rush, as though he'd been holding the words in his mouth all this time and they were suddenly escaping, 'It's only because I didn't want to do it.'

'Do what?' Officer Peterson asked quickly.

'Nothing,' he said.

'Tiber,' Mum said softly. 'Just tell us what happened.'

'Your mum's right,' said Officer Rawley. 'It will help you if you can just tell us what happened.'

'Nothing,' Tiber said again.

I could hear it in his voice now – the stubbornness set in. He wouldn't say anything to the police officers, whatever they said to him. Once, when we were playing hide-and-seek, Tiber wouldn't tell me where he'd hidden. I had looked for him everywhere. In the end I shouted out that I was giving up and went to watch television with Dad.

Not long afterwards Tiber had sauntered down the stairs, a swagger to his step. I begged and begged him to tell me where he had been, but he refused. After a while Dad had put an end to it and told me to go and find something else to do. 'He won't tell you now, love,' he had said. 'Can't you hear it in his voice? His mind is made up.'

'Tiber?' Officer Rawley said. 'We would like to ask you some more questions about this down at the station. Will you come voluntarily?'

Tiber didn't answer.

'It would really be in his best interests if he came willingly,' the policewoman said to Mum.

'Tiber? Do you hear what these police officers are saying? This is serious.'

Tiber shrugged. Mum knew it was as close to a yes as she was going to get.

'And can you come with him?' Officer Rawley asked. 'He needs to have an appropriate adult present.'

'Yes,' said Mum. 'But my daughter . . .'

'*We* can appoint another appropriate adult, but it would be better if it was you. Can you arrange for someone to look after your daughter?'

'There's no—' Mum started to say. 'Hold on. Give me a minute, will you? Leelu?'

I ran down the stairs so fast that for a moment I wondered if I would trip and fall. I forgot to open my bedroom door and pretend I was in there and just ran; ran to where everyone was standing in a small circle. Tiber was with Officer Peterson, his head low, bowed down, defeated. He didn't meet my stare.

'Leelu, come with me,' Mum said. She held my hand tightly; too tightly.

'Tiber!' I called out as she marched me out of the house. 'Tibe—'

She knocked on the front door of Betsy's house.

Mum gripped my hand firmly as we heard movement behind the door. I could see that she had started to cry. The tears ran silently down her cheeks. She wiped them away roughly with her other hand, and then, when we heard the door opening, she dropped my hand quickly so she could use both of hers to wipe her face fiercely.

Then she grabbed hold of my hand again: as the door opened, that was how we were standing, hand in hand, with Mum's face a little shiny from the tears.

'Maria?' Mum asked, a little uncertainly.

'Come in, come in.' It was Betsy's grandmother; I'd not properly met her before. She looked quite old, but not as old as Bo. She had caramel-coloured hair that was wavy and springy and wiry, sitting up, away from her head. She was wearing a long T-shirt with a cartoon cat on it.

'We can't come in. But . . . can I ask you a huge favour?'

'Favour?' she said. I could see from her face that she didn't understand.

'Can you help me?' Mum said urgently.

'Help? Sure,' Maria said. She smiled. Some of her teeth were missing but it made her smile seem kinder somehow. 'What can I do?'

'Please, can you look after Leelu? Can she stay with you? Can you look after her? It won't be for long,' Mum said. 'We are having some trouble and I need to go.'

'Sure, sure,' Maria said, still smiling toothily. 'Leelu? Come in. You hungry?' she asked me as Mum half pushed and she half pulled me in.

'I'll be as quick as I can,' I heard Mum say, and then the door slammed behind me. It was over too quickly and Mum was gone.

'Come, come,' Maria said to me. 'Betsy? Betsy?' She had to shout over the sound of the music, which filled the small hallway.

She herded me into the sitting room, where there were lots of kids jumping on the sofa in time to the music. There seemed too many to count, but later on I realized there were only six.

'Leelu!' Betsy clattered down the stairs towards me. 'What's happened? Why you here?'

'It's Tiber,' I told her. 'He's in trouble – the police are here. They're taking him now. I didn't even get a chance to speak to him.'

Betsy grabbed me by the hand and pulled me out of the front door again.

Tiber was getting into the police car. Mum was behind him, looking around anxiously. She noticed me and her mouth opened as though she was going to shout out something like, *Go back inside* or *Shut the door*, but she didn't. She gave me a funny little wave with her arm only half raised, as though she was too embarrassed to do it properly.

Tiber did not look at me at all. I heard the police car start up. They were about to drive away.

'Tiber,' I murmured. I suddenly remembered how Dog hung his head when he was worried he had done something wrong. That was what Tiber reminded me of, sitting in the police car. But Dog had never done anything wrong; it was normally just an accident that he thought he was to blame for.

I ran over to the police car and banged my hand hard against Tiber's window. He jumped and turned his head but, seeing me, quickly dropped his eyes.

'Tiber!' I shouted. 'You didn't do anything wrong, did you? You must tell them what happened.'

As the police car drove away, I felt Betsy link her arm through mine and I leaned towards her.

'Don't worry, Leelu,' she said to me. 'We will find a way to help Tiber. I have an idea.'

34

Betsy and I had a plan.

We were going to wait until her grandmother fell asleep in front of the television and then sneak over to Bo's house. Her grandmother was keeping a close eye on us both, probably because Mum had been so upset, so we would have to wait a while.

'Bo can help with his wonders, with his powers. He can do something,' Betsy said confidently.

We waited a long time. Maria was watching a programme that never seemed to end, and then, when it had finished and we thought we'd be able to leave, there was a knock on the door and some of Betsy's aunties appeared. We waited and waited, hovering on the landing and hiding in Betsy's bedroom, until finally everyone had left, Maria had shut herself in her bedroom and the house was still.

But when we were finally able to go round, we found that Bo's front door was shut.

I frowned when I saw the door. In my head, it had been left open, waiting for us to arrive.

I knocked on it gently and poked my fingers through the letter box. I thought I could make out a faint light coming from the end of the hall, but when I looked again, I couldn't be sure.

'Bo? Dog?' I called softly through the letter box. 'It's us.'

Nothing.

'Have you got something you could use?' Betsy asked.

I reached into my pocket, but I realized that the acorns were all used up now.

'Dog? Bo?' I tried again, a little louder.

Then I heard a scuffling and saw Dog coming towards us, tail wagging from side to side as he loped up to the door. Behind him I saw the figure of Bo shuffling along much more slowly.

'Leelu, Betsy, it's later than never,' Bo said once he'd opened the door.

'It's . . .' I started to say. 'Tiber's been . . .' I tried again, but then I started to cry. There was nothing I could do to stop myself.

'You got to help us, Mr Bo,' Betsy said.

'Come in, come in.' Bo ushered us inside and we settled in the peace of his sitting room, softly lit by only a couple of candles. They cast flickering shadows on walls that seemed to crowd in around us, as though they too wanted to be part of the conversation. Bo had cleared up a lot of his piles of things from the floor.

'What's happened?' he asked.

'Leelu's brother. He's in trouble with the police,' Betsy explained.

Bo's face creased with concern. 'Police?' he said.

'Can you do something?' she asked.

'I don't know,' Bo said uncomfortably. 'That would need a lot of power, and the truth is, I've almost run out. I'm almost out of wonders.'

'Can't we get some more?' Betsy said.

'But Bo is trying to get back home, to the place, and if he can't get there, then . . .' My voice petered out.

'No more wonders,' Bo said loudly. 'And no more home.'

We all fell silent.

'There has to be another way,' Betsy insisted. 'Another way back. What did you say? It is far away or it is close, depending on where you are?'

Bo scrunched up his face so his nose was wrinkled and squashed. 'There might be another way. I've been getting a feeling about something – now, I don't know if it will work, of course, a horse.'

'Bo, how is there another way? Can it really work?' I asked.

'It's only an inkling, Leelu. It might not work. We need to go outside.'

'Let's try, let's try,' Betsy said, racing towards the door.

We ran outside, Bo following us more slowly, and almost collided with Mum and Tiber, who were walking with tired, plodding steps towards our house.

Mum had a hand on Tiber's shoulder, as though worried that he wouldn't be able to walk in a straight line to the door; that he might topple over.

'Mum!' I shouted. 'Tiber!'

I threw my arms around them; I was so glad to see them. But Mum did not return my hug. She released Tiber and held me too by my shoulders, away from her so that she could look directly into my eyes.

'Leelu? Betsy? Why did you just come out of that house?' she asked.

35

I was in Big Trouble.

Even though I wasn't arrested or taken to the police station or anything like that, it was like I was in more trouble than Tiber.

When Mum found out that Betsy and I had been going to Bo's, her nostrils flared so much that I was sure smoke would come out of them.

She banned me from seeing Betsy, saying she was a bad influence, and marched Betsy back to her house. She banged her fist against the door so hard that I was sure she was going to break it.

'Maria, did you have any idea that the girls were off doing who knows what at this time of night?' she asked when Betsy's grandmother appeared.

Maria opened her mouth in astonishment, making me think of a goldfish gulping for air, but before she could speak Mum had already started up again.

'Anything could have happened to them. *Anything.* Thankfully I found them before this nonsense got any worse. Leelu will not be coming round any more – no more playing football, no more hanging out. That's it. If you do see my daughter with Betsy, I trust that you will tell me immediately.'

When Maria did speak, it wasn't in the harsh shouting tone Mum had used; it was ever so soft, almost like a murmur.

'Betsy, Betsy,' she said.

I wasn't sure if it was in disappointment or sadness, but when I looked at my friend, I saw that Betsy – Betsy, who'd rather kick a ball than talk about her feelings; Betsy, who'd stand up to all her brothers even though she was half their size; Betsy, who wasn't afraid of anyone, not even her father, whose anger was so great that it controlled him – had begun to cry.

'Say goodbye, Leelu,' Mum said.

'Betsy, I—' I managed to say before I was dragged away. The last thing I saw as Mum pulled me back into our house was Betsy's face, so crumpled with tears that for a moment I couldn't remember what she looked like when she was not crying.

As soon as we got back Mum kept on asking me why I'd thought it was all right to visit Bo.

'What have I told you about strangers?' she said. 'Anything could have happened, Leelu. *Anything*. This isn't like you.'

'He's my friend,' I tried to say. 'He needs—'

'He's most certainly *not* your friend,' Mum cut in. 'Absolutely not. I forbid it.'

'But, Mum—' I said.

'No. No,' Mum said. 'No buts. You must never go there again, do you understand?'

'But Dog needs—'

'Leelu! Enough! Things are changing around here. No more sneaking out. No more spending time in strangers' houses. No more hanging out on street corners.' Mum looked meaningfully at Tiber. 'Things are going to be . . . different.'

Tiber looked tired. His eyes seemed to droop even when he looked up at Mum; his skin was greyish. I had no words for Mum any more; she wouldn't have listened to anything anyway. I stamped upstairs to my bedroom, making each step louder than the last, and only when I'd closed the door behind me did I let myself crumple into a ball. Making myself small, wishing myself in another time and space, one where I could see my friends, one where we could be together.

'What happened at the police station?' I asked Tiber when he came to bed.

'I don't really want to talk about it,' he said quietly.

'Are you going to keep seeing them?'

'Who?'

'The boys – your friends. The ones who chased me.'

'You know they wouldn't have hurt you,' Tiber said in a rush. 'It was just a bit of fun, you know? A joke. I had no idea you could run that fast, though.'

I didn't answer.

'But no, I won't be. Mum says I can't see them any more. She says she's changing her job so she'll be in all the time. So she'll know what's going on. But anyway, after what happened I won't be able to go back to them. I failed.'

'Failed at what?'

'It doesn't matter,' said Tiber. 'It's over now.'

'So Mum won't be working nights any more?'

'That's what she says.'

Mum meant what she'd said to Tiber. The next day she told her boss that she wouldn't be coming back to work – for family reasons.

'There, that's done,' she said when she got off the phone. 'I told you that things would be different. No more staying out all night, no more wandering off. We are going to stick together from now on.'

I felt like there was a part of me that was missing. I knew that I was just the same really. I looked the same when I saw myself in the mirror. My voice sounded no different. I went to school like I always did, putting one foot in front of the other, doing what was asked of me without question until it was time to leave again. But I ached with missing Betsy and Bo. I felt it like a hole that gaped and widened with each heartbeat.

There were times when I forgot, and then I'd remember that I couldn't see them any more, and it took my breath away. I heard myself gasp out loud, as though I was short of air, starved of oxygen.

I told myself that I would go and see them as soon as Mum went out. If she didn't want me to, then she didn't have to know. But Mum was always there. She watched us closely and insisted we did everything together.

She made both Tiber and me talk to Dad on the phone by ourselves. Tiber went first. He headed upstairs to our bedroom and closed the door behind him.

Mum said that he needed privacy.

When he came back downstairs, his eyes were blotchy from crying. He wouldn't meet my gaze when he passed me the phone.

'Leelu?' Dad said sternly when I put it to my ear. I had rarely heard him speak to me like that before. It was like his voice had lost all its laughter. 'Your mum says you have been sneaking out of the house and going to see some stranger who no one knows. Is that true?'

'Dad, yes, but he's not some stranger to me. He's my friend. First he needed help – he'd fallen over and couldn't get up – and then, well . . . we became friends.'

I heard Dad sigh heavily. 'Sweetheart, you can't just go making friends with people like that. We don't know who this man is. You knew it wasn't the right thing to do – that's why you kept it secret from Mum, right?'

I didn't answer.

'You must promise me you won't go round there again,' Dad continued.

'But, Dad, he needs help. Dog—'

'Leelu, you are probably right: he might need help. But you are not going to be the one to give it to him, OK?'

'But you always say that you must help someone if you can.'

I couldn't count the number of times Dad had told us this. I could see him now, sitting across the kitchen table from me, our dinner plates scraped clean and pushed aside.

'If everyone helped out one other person who needs it,' Dad would say, bringing two fingertips together so they touched. 'If we all did this one simple thing, the world would be a much better place. We all have the capacity to do it. We all have the power in us to make a tiny difference, or sometimes a big one. It's about being brave enough to take that step.'

When Dad spoke like this, it made me feel like my chest was swelling, like there was something inside me that he was talking to.

'You always tell us, Dad – we must help someone—'

But Dad interrupted me. 'No, Leelu, this is not one of the times when you must help if you can. You are only a child. It's not up to you. Do you understand? You must not go round there again. You need to look after your brother and your mother. Concentrate on that. You need to keep each other strong.'

'But when will we be together again?' I asked. 'When are you coming over? When are you going to start looking after us? Are you going to be here next week? Or the week after?'

'Leelu, it's not as simple as that,' Dad said, his voice shifting uneasily. 'You know I would be there if I could.'

'No,' I said back. 'I think if you really wanted to be here, then you would.'

'It's not that simple,' Dad said again. 'You know that. With my work—'

There was a crackle on the phone, and I could hear his voice begin to distort and then to fade.

I didn't wait for the connection to be lost.

I hung up as I heard fragments of Dad's voice trying to get through from wherever he was now, without us.

36

I couldn't stop thinking about Bo waiting for us.

He'd be wondering why we hadn't come round, why I wasn't helping with Dog like I'd promised. But there was never a chance to go and explain: Mum was always in the house now.

I felt so angry with her for not listening to me, not hearing me, not understanding. I stayed up in the bedroom as much as I could, only coming down when I was called to come and eat. Over dinner I wouldn't speak. I would chew on mouthful after mouthful until my plate was empty, and then go back to the bedroom.

I could feel Mum's eyes following me as I silently washed up my plate and glass and made my way up the stairs again. It seemed like she wanted to say something, like the words were there in her mouth, but she couldn't let them go, couldn't let them out. I turned away from her gaze, ignoring the feeling of sickness that came over me at these times, and thought of Bo, sitting alone on the other side of the wall. Wondering why it was that we hadn't been round.

I'd begged Mum not to speak to him. The moment we ran into her and Tiber, Betsy had slammed Bo's front door closed behind us, and somehow we'd managed to shepherd Mum away from his house. She'd threatened to knock on his door the next morning, but I'd pleaded with her not to. I couldn't stop crying and shaking at the thought of it; I knew it would upset him. I knew Mum would shout. In the end she agreed she wouldn't, if only to stop my hysterical pleas and cries.

'I'll never go back,' I promised. 'I won't see him again.'

I felt myself go blank at the thought, but I kept my hands in my pockets. One wrapped around the old walnut, the other with crossed fingers, undoing the promise before I'd finished making it.

Mum hadn't found another job yet, but she said she wasn't even going to look at anything that wasn't during school hours. She and Tiber had made some kind of pact. Neither of them ever told me what had happened at the police station that night, but I could tell that they had forgiven each other in some way.

It wasn't quite like normal. They didn't joke around as they had before. In fact sometimes, when I heard serious adult voices talking, I thought Dad was there, but when I went into the room, I just saw Mum and Tiber talking quietly together. Now that Tiber was the same height as Mum, they looked each other directly in the eye.

They spoke more than Mum and I did now.

I wondered if we would ever all speak to each other again. It seemed like a very long time since we'd shared anything, the three of us, without something stirring, unspoken, just under the surface.

If I ever heard Betsy and her brothers playing outside, I'd always look out of the window, and Betsy would always be looking for me too. We'd wave and grin at each other, and she would mime something about football that I couldn't quite understand. It wasn't the same as seeing each other like we used to, but at least we were in contact.

I didn't see Bo at all.

A few days after Mum left her job I was walking back from school in between Mum and Tiber; as I passed the bin and the lamppost, I had an idea. Suddenly I knew how I could tell Bo what was happening. I would leave him a message using our old hiding spot, the space between the bin and the lamppost.

I wrote to him that night.

> *Dear Bo,*
>
> *It's Leelu. I can't come and see you any more. I can't see Betsy either. My mum found out that we were coming to see you and now she won't let me come any more. She's very angry with me even though I told her that you were my friend.*
>
> *If I do get the chance, I WILL COME BACK. I haven't forgotten you or our promise to help you fly home, back to the place. I hope Dog is all right. Tell him I'm sorry about the walks. I hope your aches are better and you can walk him now.*
>
> *Any luck with flying?*
>
> *Your friend,*
> *Leelu*
>
> *P.S. I found this stone I thought you'd like. It's not a wonder but I think you will like the colour.*

It was the kind of letter that didn't seem to say enough or say it in the right way, even though it was full of words – I had filled a whole page with writing.

I had to fold the piece of paper about five times so that it would fit into the matchbox that had once held the moss. If I used that, Bo would recognize it straight away. I also tucked in a little stone I'd picked up on my way home from school. It was caramel coloured, like a piece of buttery fudge, and shaped a bit like a cube.

The next morning, before Mum and Tiber had come out of the house I quickly wedged the matchbox between the bin and the lamppost. I brushed my fingers across it, testing that it was securely in place.

'Leelu! Away from that rubbish bin!' Mum's voice pierced the still street.

'Find this, Bo. Find this,' I whispered, looking over at the jaded blue door. The numbers looked browner and rustier than ever.

Later that day I ran ahead of Mum and Tiber, my eyes fixed on the hiding place.

Only when I was a few steps away did I see what was there. The matchbox was gone and had been replaced by a small wooden box tied up with a shoelace that had been knotted several times.

I had to tug hard to release it and, without looking at it, I buried it in my school bag among my reading books so Mum wouldn't see it.

'Leelu, why are you always hanging out by those smelly bins?' Mum said. 'Come on, get inside now.'

Once we were in she pulled the door firmly shut behind us and then locked it with a key, which she dropped into her pocket.

'Locked up for the night, are we, Mum?' Tiber said.

'Got to stop you two escaping,' she said, smiling, although her face had fallen into what looked more like a grimace.

'It's like we're in jail,' Tiber said.

'Rather this jail than another,' Mum said, and after that Tiber fell silent. He loped upstairs, taking the steps three at a time.

'I think I might have a shower, Leelu,' Mum said. 'Have you got homework to do?'

I nodded and dumped my bag on our small sagging sofa. I took out one of the books and pretended to be studying it closely, but I wasn't really reading it.

As soon as Mum had gone upstairs I pulled the wooden box out of my bag and slipped off the shoelace. Inside was a folded square of paper, along with a single feather that was light brown in colour.

I feverishly unfolded the piece of paper.

Time to go to the place.

That was all Bo had written.

37

We hadn't been able to speak to Dad for a while.

When we phoned his number, it didn't even ring. We just got the same answerphone message. It was one of those messages with a cold-sounding woman's voice, apart from the very first bit, which had Dad saying his name.

'*Adefemi Olawale . . .*' I heard, and then the woman would start up: '*. . . can't take your call.*'

Adefemi Olawale can't take your call.

I listened to it over and over.

I rang his number whenever I could so as to hear the sound of his voice. Even hearing him say those two words made me feel better.

'You've got to stop it,' Tiber told me off. 'You're using up all my credit.'

No one else seemed as worried as me that we hadn't spoken to him for a while.

One night when, once again, I hadn't got through to him and had been unable to sleep and there happened to be a full moon, I was looking at the crater that Dad had pointed out to me all those months ago. I stared and stared at it. There was something beautiful about its shape. I kept seeing different things it could be: a leaf, the curve of a bird's wing, a teardrop.

At that time of night it was quiet, or as quiet as it could be in the city. I could still make out the soft hum of traffic, a far-off siren, but mostly it was peaceful. As though the trees, buildings and roads knew it was time to sleep.

The sound of footsteps on the pavement outside broke the peace; someone sounded like they were in a hurry, their heavy steps growing louder as they came closer.

I expected them to go on past, dissolving into the night, but then came the sound of banging.

Banging on our front door.

Banging so loud that it seemed to shake the walls of our bedroom.

'Tiber?'

'Shush, Leelu.' Tiber was out of bed, standing in the shadows in the middle of the room. 'Someone's at the front door. Mum's just got up. Stay where you are.'

The banging came again. It was powerful, insistent and loud.

'Who's there?' I heard Mum call out.

'You know who it is,' the voice shouted. It sounded familiar somehow, but I couldn't place it. 'I warned you. Open this door.'

I heard the clicks as Mum unlocked it.

'Why is she letting him in?' I got out of bed and stood next to Tiber; I felt safer near him.

'It's our landlord,' Tiber said.

I recognized the voice now, though it sounded thicker than it had the day he'd shown us around the house. Much more like a snarl.

'I told you I would come round if you didn't pay up,' I heard him shout. 'Give me everything you can now. Or you are out on the streets tonight.'

'Please, please,' I heard Mum say. 'I'm getting a new job, the money is coming. It won't be long now.'

'Now. I don't care about your excuses. It needs to be now. Do I look like I am a stupid man? Do I? Do I look stupid to you?'

'This is all I have – this is everything we've got. Take it, take it,' I heard Mum say. Her voice was shaking; it was small and fearful.

'This is everything? You're in trouble if this is it. It's nowhere near enough.'

'Just a few more days – just a few more days. I'll have it, I promise.'

'End of the week. The full amount. Got it? No more excuses.'

There was the desperate sound of Mum slamming the door shut and the scrape of keys as she tried to get the right one into the lock.

And after that we heard Mum running back up the stairs. Tiber and I both flew back to our beds and I threw the duvet over my head just as Mum opened our bedroom door.

I could hear her breathing. In, out, in, out. It went like that. It sounded like she was panting, like she does after she's had to run to catch the bus.

She stayed in our bedroom, just standing there, for ages. I couldn't see her because I kept my eyes tightly closed, but I could tell that she was still there. I concentrated on keeping still. I tried to make my breaths heavy and regular like I was sleeping. I imagined Tiber doing the same, but he was always a better actor than me.

Then I heard Mum walk towards me; I could feel her pressing the duvet around me like she used to so that I was nice and cosy and all tucked in.

I should have felt warm and safe, there in my little bed by the window, with the duvet wrapped around me. But I didn't.

After that Mum left the room. I heard Tiber turn over onto his back. I waited for him to speak but he kept quiet.

'What are we going to do?' I whispered.

'We have to find some way of getting that money,' he muttered back, under his breath.

'Mum might find a job. She could do it.'

'It's not as easy as that, Leelu.'

'Or Dad could send us some money.'

'He would have done that by now if he could,' Tiber snapped.

'We should call him. He'll help, I know he will,' I said.

'No,' Tiber said, his voice as hard as stone.

I ignored him, imagining Dad coming to our rescue. 'He might come over if he knows we need his help.'

'Leelu!' Tiber hissed. I could tell that he would have shouted if he wasn't trying to keep quiet. 'You've got to give this up! Dad's not going to save us. We're going to have to do it ourselves. *We* have to make it happen.'

'But what *is* going to happen, Tiber?'

My voice had begun to tremble, just as Mum's had. I imagined the three of us standing by the bin that Mum hated so much, all our belongings around us, getting mixed up with the things that had been dumped there. Where would we go? Where would we sleep?

'I think I know a way of getting the money,' Tiber said quietly.

'How? What are you going to do?'

'Don't ask too many questions,' he told me. 'You don't want to know the answers.'

There was a bad feeling rising up inside me like a sickness. 'Talk to Mum first, please. Or Dad. They might have some money coming. We don't know.'

'It's not coming, Leelu. Not from Mum; definitely not from Dad. We'd have the money to pay for this place if Mum hadn't left her job,' Tiber said.

'She can find another one,' I said, although I could hear the doubt creeping into my voice.

'Not working only when we're at school,' Tiber said. 'She'll have to go back to working nights. She won't do that. I think she'd rather we were kicked out than do that again.' His voice sounded hard.

'What are you going to do?' I asked again. 'Tiber, you aren't going back to those friends, are you? You said you couldn't now.'

Tiber didn't answer, but I heard him turn and shift in his bed; it creaked beneath him.

'Tiber?'

But then I heard Mum's footsteps approaching and our door opened. I fell silent and pretended to be asleep.

Once she'd left I questioned Tiber again.

But he didn't want to answer me.

38

As I lay there in the darkness, sleep far from me now, I started thinking about everything that had happened since we arrived.

I remembered saying goodbye to Dad at the airport. The last time I saw his face he was smiling, but his eyes were straining towards us as though he wanted to reach out and scoop us all up in his arms.

I remembered how cold it had seemed when we stepped out of the aeroplane. At the time I didn't know that it wasn't actually that bad. It was nothing like the bone cold of winter that I was always wrapping myself up against now.

I conjured up the night we had first come to this house. Walking from one blank room to another; the unremitting feeling of being cast adrift. By then I was so tired I didn't think I'd ever know what it was like to feel rested again.

Tiber and I had argued about the bed and Mum had done the coin toss. I'd clenched the walnut, the very first wonder Bo had given me, making sure that I won. It was so that I could look at the moon, I remembered; that was why I'd wanted that bed so badly. I looked through the curtains for it, but the sky was overcast; it looked heavy, leaden, as though it was bearing down on us.

I shifted in my bed. The mattress had got lumpier over time; it was hard to get comfortable. The headboard creaked, banging against the wall as it had the first time I sat down.

Being awake when everyone else is asleep can be a lonely place.

I was used to the feeling, but there were things that helped to distract me from it. I thought of Ms Doyle clapping her hands together, her moonstone rings knocking, when she saw me. Her little room, full of exciting things to look at and read, where time passed so much more quickly than anywhere else in the school.

I thought of Betsy; how she'd play with her brothers, better at football than any of them. And Bo, of course. I thought of Bo delighting in his treasures, flying in the sitting room. These memories made me feel tremendously happy.

Bo had once said that he was glad it was me who found the wonders. He made me feel special for noticing them and for using them in the way I had. I remembered the day Bo had made the feathers fly and I'd made the leaves twirl for Betsy.

I reached into the pocket of my trousers. It was so cold when I got into bed that night that I'd put on my school trousers to warm myself up. I found the walnut, the first gift from Bo. I clasped it in my hand and pulled my duvet around me snugly. Finally a wave of sleepiness lapped over me. I yawned, feeling myself sink deeper into my lumpy old mattress. It almost felt comfortable.

I could feel myself drifting off, my head and neck wonderfully heavy and cushioned on my pillow. I tried to forget our landlord's snarling voice, the troubles that weighed us down like the thick overhanging clouds in the sky that night.

And then, just like someone had thrown on a light switch, I knew what I needed to do to make everything right again. My eyes flickered open for a moment and then closed tightly, and I fell into a deep sleep.

When the morning came, I woke with a start. The walnut was still in my hand, my fingers wrapped around it.

I sat up quickly. I remembered what I'd thought of last night; what would fix everything.

I needed to see Bo.

It was time we went to the place together.

39

The school day passed slowly, as though it knew I was desperate for it to reach its end.

I was planning on sneaking round to Bo's as soon as Mum and Tiber went to bed. Tiber was usually asleep by eleven, and Mum not long after. I just had to make sure I got the key for the front door without Mum noticing.

But I still had hours of school to go.

I tried to stop watching the clock; I'm sure its hands slowed when I did. Mrs Winters caught me staring at it and asked me if I was all right.

I nodded tightly and Mrs Winters looked like she was going to say something more, but just then there was a scuffle in the corner and two boys started fighting over their pencils. She left to go and speak to them.

We had PE outside, even though the air was so cold it hurt to breathe it in. I stamped my feet and jogged on the spot as Betsy and I had done to warm up when we met after school.

Mrs Winters produced a net sack of footballs – to a roar of excitement – and divided us up into groups to pass the balls to each other. We hadn't played football at school before, and for once I felt like I had a head start. As Betsy had taught me, I stopped the ball with my foot and then set it spinning to the person next to me.

I had to wait a while for my next turn because Terri missed the ball completely and had to run over to the other side of the playground to retrieve it.

After we'd done this for most of the lesson, Mrs Winters blew her whistle and we gathered around her.

'We've got time for a short game before we finish,' she told us.

There was another whoop of excitement.

We were divided into teams, and then there was a scrum and a scramble for the ball, and someone fell over and the whistle was blown again.

I hung back.

Drew had the ball and was almost surrounded when he spotted me, free, a little way from him.

'Leelu!' he shouted, and before he was engulfed by the crowd, he kicked the ball towards me.

It was a good pass, though not as good as Betsy's, but I ran towards the ball and dribbled it towards the goal. One of the taller girls, Aisha, ran straight at me; I kicked the ball so it sped round and past her. Then I ran to catch up with it.

I heard someone shouting something, but no one was telling me to stop and so I kept going towards the goal. Two boys were running towards me – I could hear their feet thudding hard on the ground like a kind of countdown.

Betsy and I had been practising sending the ball up into the air using our feet, and I felt sure I could do it – although Betsy had told me it was hard to do it in a game. It was one of our tricks; at first I had found it easier than Betsy. It made me think of Bo flying.

I concentrated on the ball; it rolled and skidded easily along the ground and, as I looked at it, it seemed as though the world around me – the kids, Mrs Winters, Mum, Tiber, Dad, my worries and my dreams, all of it – was just a bit further away. For that moment all that mattered was the ball in front of me, the force within my legs that drove it on towards the goal. I positioned the ball between my feet and then flicked them upwards so that it soared high into the air.

It flew up.

Over the heads of the boys.

Up, up, up it went.

A neon-orange moon against the white, overcast sky.

I ran round to catch up with it, but by then no one was chasing me any more. It was as though everyone else had stopped. Not even the goalkeeper, a boy called Mehmet, moved as I dribbled the ball into the goal.

They weren't chasing me because they were shouting.

'Leelu! Leelu! Leelu!' in a chant.

'How did you do that?' Terri came running over to me. 'Can you teach me?'

I was so unused to anyone asking me anything, I didn't answer at first.

Terri sighed, her eyes wide and watching. 'I forgot, you don't speak,' she said quietly.

All of a sudden my mouth opened, and before I knew it I had answered her.

'I can speak,' I said.

My voice rang out clear and strong. As Bo's did when he talked about the place. As Betsy's did when she spoke about football.

The children who were standing nearby looked up, astounded. Their mouths hung open.

'But you never ... You've never ...' Terri started to splutter.

'I know,' I said. I looked around at my classmates, finally meeting their eyes. Some smiled at me cautiously. Others still looked shocked. 'I guess ... I was scared.'

It was such a relief to say it, to admit to it after all the time that had passed, that I felt like laughing out loud. Despite everything that was happening with Mum and Tiber, there was a giddiness within me that rose up like a bird stretching out its wings and soaring into the blue of the sky.

Then there was another voice.

'I was scared when I first started here too,' Aisha said.

I turned to her in astonishment; she was one of the loudest girls in the class. She looked at me shyly from beneath her fringe, which was swept to one side in an artful wave. 'I joined last year, Leelu. I haven't been here that long either,' she told me, her dark eyes shining a little. And then she turned to everyone else. 'You all knew each other so well – you'd already made friends. It was really lonely at first.'

'I'd never have thought it,' said one of the boys. I realized that it was Drew – the boy who had seen me in the book corner that first day – who'd passed the ball to me. 'You were so loud.'

'Well, I was hiding it, wasn't I?' Aisha said. 'If I talked all the time, then who would know?'

'I guess I was hiding it in a different way,' I said.

Aisha grinned at me.

'I think we thought you didn't like us,' Terri said slowly.

'No, it wasn't that,' I said. 'I just felt so different to you. You all know what you're doing all the time. With the work and everything. I felt . . . well, a bit stupid with it all, really.' Now that I had started talking I wondered if there was anything I wasn't scared to say. I could feel everyone looking at me, but this time it didn't make me feel uncomfortable or awkward. I glanced up at them, meeting their stares.

Finally Drew spoke. 'That's not true. I don't know what I'm doing all the time. Sometimes I don't get it.'

The others nodded in agreement and I heard them murmuring, 'No, me neither.'

'I'm not sure I'll ever understand what a frontal adverbial is,' Terri said. She chuckled. 'Poor Mrs Winters. She spends so long on them, but I still have no idea what they are.'

'Maybe we're not so different after all,' Aisha said.

'Perhaps not,' I said quietly before Mrs Winters blew the whistle again and told us we'd better hurry up and get changed.

'A lot of voices over here,' she said. 'Let's walk in nice and quietly so as not to disturb the other classes.'

Drew groaned a little. Aisha raised her eyebrows at Terri and me, a suggestion of a grin on her lips.

And Mrs Winters looked at us all, her eyes travelling from face to face.

And then she started smiling too, and went off to the other side of the line, where she wouldn't be able to hear us talking.

40

That day I dashed out of school feeling like I might be able to take off and fly if I ran fast enough.

My worries for Bo, my fears for Tiber, missing Dad – none of it seemed so dreadful now. There was a lightness in every step I took, as though my shoes were made of something different, something that made me taller.

I'd spoken to Terri and Aisha and some of the others in my class a bit more. When we'd finished our work, Mrs Winters said we'd all done well that week and could have a bit of free time until school finished, so long as we didn't get too noisy.

They had lots of questions for me. Aisha wanted to know where I used to live and Terri wanted to know where I lived now. Drew asked me if I liked football and Hassan wanted to find out if I had any brothers or sisters.

I told them a little bit about Tiber, a little about Mum, a little about Betsy.

When no one could overhear us, Aisha asked me about Dad.

'I don't see my dad any more,' she told me. 'That's one of the reasons we moved here. He's not allowed to know where we live. He's got problems, Mum says.'

'Do you think you'll ever see him again?' I asked.

'I'm not sure. I used to think I would. But now I'm not so sure.' She shrugged quickly as though shaking something off. 'But my mum's happier now they're not together any more. That's a good thing. How about you? When do you think you'll see your dad? When is he coming over?'

'Well, they used to say he was coming soon. But no one mentions him coming now. Dad doesn't talk about it. My mum gets cross if I ask too many questions.'

Aisha nodded her head slowly, her eyes thoughtful.

I decided to talk to Mum again. I would be calm. I would speak to her in a way that would make her listen. I'd ask if Dad was all right. I'd find out if there was a problem with his work. I'd tell her that if he didn't come over, I'd be all right, I'd be OK, but we needed to know what was going to happen.

There were so many things that were unspoken and that I was scared to ask about, but I knew now that talking was a way of mending things; a special kind of wonder that made things happen.

It was as though I'd been wearing glasses that made everything murky, blurred their outlines, cast everything in shadow so that I couldn't see things properly. But now that I had taken them off, I could see everything for what it was. There were problems, but we could make them better, we could start to fix them, if only we spoke to each other honestly about them.

I would tell Mum that we had overheard the landlord. That we needed to make a plan together because Tiber wanted to do something and I was worried about what that might be. I'd explain, properly this time, about Bo and what he was like. How much he had helped me; how much I needed to help him. She'd understand how important it was for us to visit him.

It felt like a dazzling, burning secret that I was carrying around with me, and at home time I rushed out of the classroom, Aisha and Terri beside me, still in shock and awe that I was now talking; it was as though they wanted to stick by me to make up for lost time, or maybe to check that I wouldn't clam up again. We raced down the stairs together, two at a time, and by the time we got to the bottom we were breathless with laughter, our legs throbbing, but not in a painful way.

'I've got to find my mum,' I said to them, my words coming out in gasps.

'See ya next week,' Terri said.

'Next week,' I said, and for once I liked the sound of that. Next week at school.

'Have a good weekend, Leelu,' said Aisha.

'You too,' I said back before I ran out of the door.

But Mum wasn't waiting outside like she usually was. I walked around a bit, ducking past crowds of parents, children running past me in that free, wild kind of way that marked the end of the week. I felt like that too, but I was worried when I couldn't find Mum.

There was no sign of her.

I saw Catherine, the mother I'd met on my very first day. She was looking at a painting one of her sons had thrust into her hands.

'Yes, I can see that's Mary Seacole, Daniel. It's very convincing,' she was saying as I walked past. 'All right there, Lou? How are you?'

'Hi, Catherine,' I said. 'I'm just looking for my mum.'

She looked around. 'I haven't seen her today actually. Are you OK getting home? You could have Mrs Charlton call her from the office.'

'I'll be OK,' I assured her. 'I know the way home.' Before I left, I turned to her again. 'Catherine?'

'Yes, Lou?'

'I'm sorry I didn't tell you before, but my name's actually Leelu, not Lou. I didn't know how to tell you earlier.'

'Leelu,' Catherine said thoughtfully. 'You know, that really does suit you much better than Lou.' Just then, one of her sons came tearing towards her. 'Whoa, James,' she said. 'Careful!'

'Bye, Catherine,' I said, waving as she caught him before he crashed into her.

'Bye, Leelu!' she called back.

I walked back quickly, sure I'd find Mum at home. Perhaps she'd had a job interview, I told myself. Or maybe she'd seen the landlord about the money and it was all sorted out now.

But when I got there, Mum was standing by the door. She had been crying. When she saw me, she began to run towards me and I thought for a moment that we were going to collide, just as Catherine and her son had after school. In a way we did. Mum reached out and drew me to her in a close hug. Her arms wrapped tightly around me. I could hear the beating of her heart. It throbbed and pulsed, and I could feel its vibrations against my cheek.

'I'm sorry, I'm sorry,' Mum was saying. Her voice was muffled, buried in the top of my head.

Then she pushed me away, holding me by the shoulders as though she was examining me.

'What's happening?' I asked her.

'It's Tiber,' Mum said.

She took a breath as though to steady herself, but it was very shallow. It sounded like the air was being squeezed out of her.

'He's missing.'

41

Tiber had not been to school that day.

No one had seen him since he left Mum and me that morning. Eight hours ago.

'I've been going round everywhere,' Mum said. 'Showing everyone his picture. Asking if anyone has seen him. But nothing. There's nothing.'

She held up a photo. It was one of the few we'd brought over of Dad; in this one he was with Tiber. I took it gently from her. Tiber's mouth was open, as though he was about to say something or start smiling or both. It had been taken at our neighbour's wedding. In the background you could make out a blur of brightly coloured outfits, and the brilliant blue of the sky framed Tiber's face.

I'd taken the photograph. He'd told me to.

'Hey, Lulu,' Tiber had said. 'Get one of me and Dad.'

The photograph had been folded so you could only see Tiber's face, but I spread it out flat to see

Dad too. Tiber had his arm around him, but Dad wasn't looking at the camera at all, even though I remember shouting at him to.

'Look over here, Dad! Smile at the camera,' I'd commanded. But he hadn't. He was gazing at Tiber as though he couldn't believe his luck, having him for a son. With a sort of amazement. With love.

I took a deep breath. It had to start now, me changing things, making things better by being strong. I wasn't going to rely on a magical place saving us; it was up to me.

'Mum? Mum?' She was wringing her hands and talking under her breath, looking all about her as if she thought Tiber might pop out from behind a tree at any moment. Finally her desperate eyes fixed on me.

'Mum, we have to tell Dad,' I said softly. 'He needs to come now. When he knows, he'll come over. I know he will.'

Mum swelled up as though she might burst with everything she wanted to say, but then, like a balloon losing its air, she deflated. She hung her head, depleted.

'Leelu,' Mum said slowly. 'Your dad . . . Your dad's not going to be able to help. I mean, yes, we should tell him and he'll want to be here if we can't find Tiber. But he's not going to be able to come over . . . Not now, not with everything.'

If Mum had told me that at any other time during the past few months, I would have exploded. I could almost hear my voice ringing out: *What do you mean he's not coming? He is – he's coming over. You've always said he would. You both said. He is coming, he is. I won't believe he's not.*

Did I still believe that, if I thought about it hard enough, I could undo what Mum had said, that I could make him come over just by wanting it badly enough, just by the power of thought? I used to think that.

Instead, I stopped myself. I fell quiet, absorbing Mum's words. I stood very still and looked down at the pavement. My feet were facing inwards, towards each other, and a few leaves rested next to them. They were a russet, golden brown, a glorious kind of colour, curled over on themselves in curves and arches. In the past I would have dismissed them as being brown-grey and dull, but now I could see that those dried-out old leaves were beautiful. Beautiful in the way that the wonders Bo had given me were beautiful.

I could feel the wind wrapping itself around me, but not in a cold way that made me shiver; it felt refreshing and cool. Bracing, revitalizing.

I looked up at Mum. 'Mum, you have to tell me – what's going on?'

'I don't know where to start,' she said, still wringing her hands, fiddling with her rings as though she wanted to take them off.

'Start at the beginning,' I said, thinking of the little phrases Bo said sometimes.

'I didn't want you to worry, but there have been things ... happening with your dad. Bad things. You know we told you about his work?'

I nodded.

'It wasn't a lie when we said he couldn't come because of it. It was about his work; it's always about his work. That ... Well, that's another problem,' Mum said, continuing to worry the rings on her fingers.

'I didn't want to have to tell you like this,' she said.

'You can tell me,' I said gently.

'Your dad ...' Mum stumbled to say the words aloud. 'Your dad's in prison.'

42

'That's why I couldn't get through to him. His phone . . .' I remembered the monotone of his voicemail.

Adefemi Olawale can't take your call.

It was telling the truth: he couldn't take the call.

'Yes, that's why we've stopped hearing from him.' Mum nodded, looking down as though studying the leaves too. 'We've been worried that it would happen for a little while. That's the real reason why we came over here. And now . . . Well, now it has.'

'But why? What did he do?'

'Your dad was saying things that people didn't like. You know what he's like . . . what a fighter he is when he sees something unjust. He started speaking out, supporting people who are homosexual; he wanted to change the law. It's a good thing he's doing, don't get me wrong, although sometimes . . . sometimes I wish he'd put us first.'

'What was the law?'

'In our country, if a man wants to marry a man, or a woman wants to marry a woman . . . they can't do it. It's very different here. You must have seen. Here, it's accepted that people are different. There are heterosexuals – a man and a woman who love each other and live together – and homosexuals – a man and a man or a woman and a woman who love each other and want to be together. And they are treated more or less the same here. Or they should be, anyway. But in our country it's not like that. Homosexuals are not allowed to be themselves. That's what your dad was speaking out about. He wants people to treat them the same.'

I thought of Dad, always telling us that we should help others if we could. I remembered how, if Tiber and I argued, he would listen to us both; only if we couldn't agree did he reach into his pocket for a penny to toss. That way it was fair to us both.

'I've heard that he might be able to get out of prison. There's an appeal, and as soon as he's out he'll come over here. He'll be safe here. He wants to continue his work from here, as best he can.'

Mum's eyes grew glassy with tears, which she wiped away impatiently.

I had the feeling that I was outside my body, watching myself take in the news Mum was giving me. I floated up above where Mum and I were standing, circling us both. I was crying – I could see my tears, the frozen look etched upon my face. And Mum, her face naked with honesty, with worry, reaching out for me.

That was what brought me back into my body, into the moment. The sight of Mum trying to reach me.

My fingers met hers and we gripped each other's hands tightly.

'I'm sorry,' Mum said, so quietly I almost didn't hear her.

I let myself remember Mum and Dad together. The photo from their wedding day hanging in the sitting room of our old house, their grins reflected in each other's faces. The quiet voices after I'd gone to bed; I couldn't hear what they were saying, but the gentle sound of them talking would always lull me to sleep.

I let myself breathe, think, take in what Mum had told me.

It was better knowing, I thought.

It was better knowing what was happening.

It was better hearing how Mum felt.

It was better finding out where Dad was and what he had been doing.

It felt like an enormous hole inside me, thinking about what was happening to Dad, but there was something else, something truthful, that made me feel a strength well up within me. It kept me from falling, kept me standing tall.

'When will Dad get out of prison?' I asked.

'I'm not sure exactly, I'm afraid. But when he does, he'll come over here as soon as he possibly can . . . Are you OK, Lulu?' Mum said, calling me the name that Tiber had appointed for me. 'I know it's a huge shock.'

I asked myself if I was OK, studied myself as though I was doing an experiment, scanning my brain for feelings and worries. I missed Dad so much, I realized. That was mostly how I felt. I missed seeing his face, hearing his laugh that made me laugh, his happy voice saying my name. But I would see him again, I knew that now.

There had been a time when I couldn't believe that it would ever be OK here without him. But I had found good things: Betsy, Bo and Dog, Ms Doyle, and Aisha and Terri, who I'd only just begun to know.

I finally understood why we had come to London; why it was that we had left behind everything we knew. It was because my dad was trying to help people. Like Mum said, he was trying to make the world a better place. Mum was right: that was something to be proud of.

'I'm OK,' I told Mum in the end. 'It's good . . . good to know the truth.'

Mum nodded and bit her lip.

Suddenly a thought occurred to me: 'Does Tiber know?'

Mum took another deep breath. This time she filled her lungs. Her shoulders rose and fell as though she was releasing something within her. 'Yes. I told him after we'd been to the police station.'

It made more sense now, the way he'd erupted when I talked about Dad last night. He knew more than he'd let on.

'It's a lot to get used to,' Mum continued. 'And it will take time. I'm sorry that we didn't tell you from the start. It would have been better if we had, perhaps. We were just doing what we thought was best.'

'I don't know,' I said. Adults always talked about doing things 'for the best', but I wondered if they'd got it wrong. Didn't we sometimes just do things because we felt there was no other way, no other path? It wasn't for the best or for the worst; it just was.

'I'm glad I know the truth now,' I said. 'I was thinking earlier that it's important to talk to each other. To listen too.'

'I think you're right,' Mum said. She wiped her face as though wiping away a tear, but although her eyes glistened, she had stopped crying. 'We need to be honest with each other. Starting from now.'

She took my hand and squeezed it, and then she looked at me, her eyes so wide that I could see my own reflection in them.

'I'm so worried about Tiber. Leelu, do you have any idea where he might be?'

43

I told Mum what Tiber and I had said to each other the night before.

'So you heard him? Mr Abenezzi? How could you not? You did such a good job of pretending to be asleep, the both of you. I thought you'd slept through.'

'Tiber said that Dad couldn't help and that you wouldn't get the money, so it was up to us. He said he had an idea—'

'Oh, Tiber!' Mum exclaimed. 'It's difficult with Dad being in prison, but I've been in touch with Uncle Ropo about what happened and he has sent us some money to help us out. You don't need to worry about the rent or about Mr Abenezzi. It's all sorted out now.'

'But Tiber doesn't know that. I think he's gone back to those friends he used to hang out with. I think he was going to try and get money from them somehow.'

'Did he say he was going to do that?' Mum asked.

I thought back to our whispered conversation. 'No, not exactly. But when I asked him, he didn't tell me he wasn't going to. He didn't deny it.'

'I just hope he's not that stupid,' Mum said. 'He knows it'll mean trouble for him. I've got to hope that he means something else; that there's some other reason why he's missing. But thank you, Leelu. I'll tell the police – it might help.'

'Are they looking for him?'

'They're not that concerned really. To them, it's not been that long. And when they asked me if he had ever taken off before and I said yes, they said that it was just a pattern of behaviour. Running away. That it happens all the time with teenagers. They think he'll come back when he's ready.'

'I'm worried too, Mum,' I said. 'I think he would be back by now if he could. It's different this time.'

'I know, Leelu, I know. I feel the same.'

We were still holding hands, and for the first time in ages I felt connected to Mum. I could almost feel it running between us, passing through her fingertips, from her palms to mine.

'I'm going back to the police station to tell them what you told me, and then I'll walk around the neighbourhood for a bit and keep looking for him. Could you stay here? Just in case he comes back?'

'Yes, of course,' I said.

'Lock the door after me, won't you?' Mum said, pressing the key into my hand. 'I'll come back soon and we'll have something to eat together, OK?'

She kissed me on the forehead and was gone.

I told myself that I would only be a few minutes, but as soon as Mum had left I let myself out of the house and knocked on Betsy's door. Maria answered after a while, but when she saw me, she just said, 'No Betsy,' and made an expression like she was sorry. I didn't know whether she meant that she wasn't there or that I wasn't allowed to see her.

I tracked back to Bo's house and knocked furiously.

'Bo!' I called through the letter box. 'It's Leelu. I'm sorry! I'm sorry!'

I saw Dog come loping up to me. He licked my fingers through the letter box and whined when I didn't come in. There was no sign of Bo.

I suddenly thought of him lying on the floor after one of his flying try-outs. I had to get the door open. I rushed back to my house and ran up to my room. I pulled the dried-out piece of bracken that Bo had given me all those weeks ago out from under the loose floorboard, and took it back to Bo's with me.

Using the bracken, I had the door open in a flash, and I dashed into the living room, looking for Bo.

But he wasn't there.

He wasn't anywhere.

44

Dog pressed his nose to mine. It felt viscous and cold.

'Where's Bo?'

He pressed his nose to me again, and this time it slid across my cheek in a smear. Then he loped towards the front door and gave a little moaning whine. He was pawing to go outside.

'Toilet, Dog?'

He wagged his tail.

'All right, we'll just go to the bins,' I told him. 'I'm sure Bo will be back soon.'

But Dog had other ideas. He started pulling me down the street, walking at first, and then trotting, faster and faster. He swung his head from side to side, sniffing the street and the air as though it was all new to him. He seemed desperate to run around and I wondered if he had missed his walk that day.

'Dog! No! We have to go back,' I told him. I didn't want Mum to come back to find me gone, and there was something about the way the shadows fell across the streets that made me shiver.

But Dog didn't listen. He pulled even harder; I had to run to keep up with him. I held on to his lead with all my strength.

'Dog! What are you doing?' He led me down one street and then another. I followed him blindly, but I soon realized that we were taking the same route that he took with Bo on their daily walk. The one we'd followed the night we saw Tiber and his gang.

When we'd turned another corner, I saw the block towering over us. This time almost all the lights were out; only a few windows were still illuminated.

It was darker tonight. I looked all around for figures in the blackness. My eyes strained for the profile of my brother, leaning back lankily, running with his long strides, but there was no one there.

When we got to the point where we'd met the group before, Dog stopped abruptly. I almost tripped over him.

'What is it, Dog?' I asked him. His ears flicked back so that they lay flat on his head.

I stroked him gently, but then I felt myself freeze.

I could hear the sound of voices.

I'd heard them before.

The same voices I'd heard when Dog and I were last here together.

They were coming from the foot of the block.

Where it was darkest.

Where it collected the most shadows.

And they were coming towards us.

45

I took a little step towards the block.

Everything was screaming at me to run away, but there was no time. We needed to hide before they found us, and there was nowhere else to go.

My hands were shaking. My breath came in gasps. Fear hunched over my shoulders as though I was wearing it; a heavy, sodden cape. It dragged me backwards; it resisted my steps.

But then I heard one of the voices call something loudly and I ran towards the block.

Some huge, cube-shaped bins on wheels stood outside and I crouched behind one so I couldn't be seen. The stone of the pavement was viciously cold and reeked of the sharp smell of urine.

I pulled Dog towards me, wrapping my arms around his rough, wiry fur. I could feel his warmth through my jumper; it steadied me a little. I ducked my head down as the voices grew louder still.

'Oi, Trip!' one of them said. 'Check this out.'

I held my breath. I closed my eyes. I was sure one of them had spotted me. My arms tightened around Dog. I felt his wet nose find mine.

'Oh yeah,' came another voice. I recognized it as the one who'd called me 'Dog Girl' before. 'That's funny. That's *really* funny.' He spoke with a confident swagger. I could almost hear everyone listening to him as he spoke: they all fell silent around him.

'That's what I said, Trip. Like, no joke, those exact words.' There was a murmur of agreement and 'Yeah's.

They were almost upon me.

I opened my eyes and saw that they were bent over a phone, looking at something on its bright screen. Its light lit up their faces in the darkness. The one I guessed was Trip looked at it with a hard glare. And all the others, they looked at Trip.

'Shall we check on the patient?' another one said.

I shrank down again. He rapped the bin as he passed by. It made a dull clunking sound that almost made me jump.

'Nah,' said Trip. 'Leave him be, leave him be.'

I put my hand to the cold metal of the bin. I knew where Tiber was. I had found him. He was inside the bin.

All I wanted to do was to jump up and wrench the lid open but they were still close by, only a few steps away. I shrank down as small as I could make myself and tried to step back a little.

I didn't see what was on the ground behind me.

There was a huge clatter as I knocked over a pile of rubbish. A glass bottle fell and smashed into pieces, piercing the air with a splintering sound that seemed to ring out long after it had finished.

'Who's there?' one of the boys shouted.

'Come out, come out,' said another.

'Show yourself,' said the hard voice of Trip.

I looked down at Dog and stroked his huge grey head. I didn't have any power left; my pockets were empty. There was nothing I could do that wasn't just me.

I unclipped Dog's lead. 'When I tell you to run, Dog, run. Run home, OK?'

The boys were still calling and taunting and threatening.

I took a deep breath and stepped out from behind the bin.

'Look who it is.'

'Dog Girl, come back for more.'

'Here for another race, Dog Girl?'

I took another step towards them. I could feel Dog pulling slightly as I held his collar.

'We're gonna catch you this time,' the one called Trip said, and as he spoke, I felt them all crowd in towards me.

'Run, Dog!' I cried. I let go of him and he bounded off, back in the direction from which we had come, back towards our street. At that exact moment I pivoted round as Betsy had taught me and ran with all my might, as though I was chasing a ball down, in the other direction.

There was just a moment when the boys didn't know who to follow. Whether to run after Dog or after me, and in that tiny moment of hesitation I sprinted away.

I ran with everything I had.

I ran so that it felt like my legs might come off.

When I glanced behind and saw that the boys were coming after me, I leaned forward and ran even faster.

I knew that if I could just get to the main street, then I would be all right. There were people there, lights, cars, shops. Protection. I wasn't sure what I would do when I got there, but I knew that if I made it there, I'd be OK.

I thought I heard the boys getting closer and closer behind me, but I didn't think my legs could go any faster. There was no forgotten walnut in my pocket, no acorn, no feather. Nothing was going to make me faster but me.

Then I heard a voice in my head. It was Betsy's: *You can do it, little fish.*

Then there was Bo's: *You really are doing tremendously well.*

Ms Doyle's: *Look what you can do when you believe in yourself.*

I put every bit of me into covering that last bit of road. I could see the lights just ahead of me, and the footsteps behind me sounded further and further away.

As soon as I reached the street I turned a corner, and there I saw a bus about to pull away. With the last of my energy I jumped through the doors as they closed, and then ducked behind the people who were standing in the aisle.

I saw the boys run out onto the street, looking around for me.

They hadn't seen me.

I was safe.

46

But of course it wasn't over.

I knew where Tiber was and I had to get back to him. They didn't know that I was his sister. They had no reason to link my being there behind the bin with what they had done to Tiber, but I didn't know what they were planning. I had to rescue him before they did anything else.

I got off the bus after a few stops and then walked back to the block another way, hiding in front gardens and behind cars if I heard anyone coming. When I got closer, I could see the boys still standing by the bins, so I tucked myself away behind a wall and listened.

They were telling Trip that they had lost me; they were still out of breath from the chase. Trip said something I couldn't hear, and then I heard their footsteps.

I looked up slowly over the wall to see them disappear into the block. The door slammed behind them, and when I stood up, the square was as empty as when I'd first arrived. I waited for a few moments, and then I dashed back to the bin, my feet light on the ground. My legs were throbbing from running; if the boys came back, I knew I wouldn't be able to outrun them again.

The bin was made of metal and had one of those tops that looks like a lid, only now I noticed that it had been tied shut. Three lines of blue rope circled it; they had been tied over and over in an elaborate knot.

He had to be in there.

I knocked it as I'd heard the boy do.

Clunk.

Clunk.

There was nothing.

'Tiber?' I said, as loudly as I dared. 'Tiber?'

No sound came from the bin.

'Tiber, it's Leelu. I'm here, I've come to get you. Please answer me.' My voice had turned wavy; I couldn't control it.

That's when I heard it.

Clunk, clunk.

An answering knock to my call. And a sound too.

I had to press my ear against the bin to hear it.

It was only a murmur. As soft as a sigh.

'Lulu.'

47

My fingers struggled with the tight coils of the knot.

The cold made them numb and stiff.

'Hang on, Tiber,' I told him. 'Hang on.'

I thought I'd never be able to undo it, but finally, finally, one rope came a little loose and I was able to pull the rest away.

It took me a couple of goes to wrench the lid open fully, and when I did, it fell open with a clang that made me look around in case anyone had heard.

He was lying underneath some flattened cardboard boxes and rubbish. There were chicken bones and takeaway boxes and plastic bags full of things like vegetable peelings and crumpled cans.

'Tiber, Tiber.' I couldn't stop crying his name, but then I heard him say, 'Shh, they might come back.' I swallowed hard and looked behind me at the door they'd disappeared through.

'Can you stand? Can you get out?'

'I'm not sure,' he said. Every word sounded like an effort.

'See if you can, Tiber. We've got to get you out.'

He managed to lift off some of the cardboard and I pulled it out. After that he could just about stand if he held on to the side of the bin for support.

'Can you do it? Should I go and get help?'

'No.' He almost shouted it. 'Don't leave. I can do it.'

It took him a couple of tries, but then he jumped high enough to get his top half out of the bin. But then he started to fall forward, out of control, head-first onto the hard stone of the pavement. I rushed to catch him and he toppled onto me. He was heavier than he looked, but neither of us was hurt. Well, not from that anyway.

Tiber didn't look like himself any more.

His face was so changed. It was distorted and thick in all the wrong places. I could see that he wouldn't be able to open his right eye even if he wanted to. All the skin around it was puffy, as though blown up like a balloon. An angry-looking cut traced all the way down his cheek. From a distance it reminded me of the winding lines that rivers make on maps. One of his arms hung limply by his side.

'Put the boxes back inside and close the lid,' Tiber told me. 'So they won't know I'm gone immediately.'

I did as he said. I remembered the way the lid hung heavily and made sure that I closed it gently so that it didn't make a sound. I kept expecting the voices to return again, and my fingers fumbled awkwardly. I tried to retie the rope around the bin but I couldn't make it look the same.

In the end it was Tiber who said, 'Leave it – let's get out of here.'

We started the slow hobble back to our house. Tiber tried to walk by himself but he kept crying out in pain. After that he leaned on me, gripping my shoulder so tightly that it hurt. We walked in unison as though we were doing some awful version of a three-legged race.

It took a long time. All the while we both kept looking behind us.

When we reached our street and the dark blue door of our house was in sight, Tiber stumbled. He lay motionless on the ground. I don't think he had anything more to give.

Dog, who'd been sitting outside Bo's house, ran over to us.

I rushed ahead to our house – I could see that the light was on – while Dog circled Tiber protectively, barking.

Mum flung open the door before I reached it. 'Leelu, what—'

But before she finished, I gasped, 'We've got him.'

She ran over to him, shouting for me to call an ambulance.

And Tiber lay there, unmoving and silent.

48

Tiber's arm was broken. It was now encased in a thick white cast that made him look even skinnier as he lay in the bed.

'Tiber?' I whispered, but he slept and did not stir.

'Leelu.' I heard Mum behind me. 'We must let him rest.'

There was only one chair. Mum said that I could sit on it while she went to find something for us to drink.

It was too big for me, so I sat with my legs folded beneath me like I had on my first day of school, so that I could reach his bedside.

'Tiber,' I said. 'I'm here. We're here.' I looked around a little self-consciously, but no one was paying any attention. 'Tiber, please wake up.'

His eyelids were so heavily bruised and swollen, I wondered if it was even possible for him to open his eyes.

'Tiber? Mum says that you are just resting and that you'll wake up, but please wake up now. Tiber?'

But there was nothing. Tiber lay as still as a statue.

'I need to know that you are all right. Tiber? Do you hear me? Tiber? Tiber?' I asked again. I thought of the old stories about enchantments that sent people to sleep. You needed to do something to rouse them. You'd say a spell or give them some special potion.

I found myself reaching into my pockets, but I had nothing left. Not one of Bo's wonders that I could use to wake him.

Instead I reached out and held his fingers – the bits that weren't covered with cast. I squeezed them gently.

'I'm here, Tiber. You're safe now,' I told him.

'Lulu?' I heard him whisper. His voice was hoarse and it sounded like a whisper. 'Is that you?'

I beamed at him. 'It's me, it's me. How are you? Are you OK?'

'Been better.' Tiber smiled, but his lips were so dry, it looked like a grimace.

'What happened?'

'It's just . . . nothing. Just an accident.'

'Tiber. You can tell me. You must. You must tell me.'

Tiber frowned and started to speak, but there was a lump in his throat and he couldn't get his words out.

'Was it to do with your idea of how to get the money?' I asked quietly. 'What happened?'

'It's . . . It's stupid . . . but, Leelu, I don't want to tell you. I don't want you to know. You're my little sister.'

'I am. I am your sister. I might be little, but I'm all you've got and I take care of you, like you take care of me. But we have to talk to each other; we have to keep talking, being honest . . . otherwise it's not real, is it? We need to know each other.'

'When did you get so wise?' Tiber smiled and gave a low chuckle, but then he winced as though it pained him and stopped.

'Tell me what happened. It will help.'

'It's so stupid,' Tiber said. 'I thought I could make it work. I went to see the friends I used to hang out with at night. Before, they wanted me to start doing stuff. You know, bad stuff. Mugging people, hurting people. The day before the police came, that was the first time. And the last, I suppose.'

'Why did you go back to them?'

'Because one of the reasons they said I should do it was . . . sometimes you get money. If someone is carrying cash or you can sell their phone on, stuff like that. I thought I could go back to them and do it, get some money.'

'But, Tiber . . . But, Tiber . . .' I couldn't put into words how wrong it was, everything he was describing. I couldn't believe he would do those things. 'Did you do it? Is that how you got hurt?'

Tiber shook his head. 'They said that I wasn't one of them any more, that I couldn't just come back like that, that I had to have an initiation. Then they started hitting me. I couldn't tell which one of them was doing the hitting – it was all of them. I couldn't get away. When I couldn't stand any more, they left me in that bin. I couldn't get out. I thought . . . I thought I might be in there for ever.' His voice died as he started to cry softly.

'You're safe now,' I told him. And I bent down and kissed his fingers.

Then Mum came back, and when she saw us, she just dropped the drinks she was holding on the floor. They spilled everywhere, making a wobbly, wavy pattern that reminded me of the bracken leaves that Bo had once given me.

She opened her arms up to us and we stayed like that, entwined with one another.

And somehow that dark, dark night passed into morning.

49

The next day we watched over Tiber.

He slept a lot. He lay so very still and quiet that I could hardly believe it was my brother at all. Tiber usually tosses when he sleeps. He turns and burrows and shakes the bed with his movements.

But not that day. He lay unmoving, apart from one of his hands, which flickered with movement. His fingers flexed and trembled to their own rhythm; little flutterings that made me think of a bird's wings beating in flight. It was the hand that I had held, almost hidden beneath the cast.

That night Mum wanted to stay with Tiber but said she thought I should get some proper sleep. She'd spoken to Maria, Betsy's grandmother, and arranged for me to stay the night with them.

As soon as we saw each other, Betsy and I hugged tightly. I was sure she would start talking about football immediately, but instead she said, 'Hey, little fish. I didn't think we see each other again.'

'Me neither,' I said.

We squeezed each other's hands.

I told her what had happened to Tiber; how I'd sprinted away from the boys. And how I'd played football at school, which had helped me to start talking to everyone.

'I knew it!' Betsy exclaimed. 'I always say football will help one day.'

'You were right,' I said, grinning.

'How's Mr Bo?' she asked.

I frowned. He still hadn't been there when I'd arrived back with Tiber. When we'd gone off in the ambulance, I'd had to leave Dog in the house alone, hoping that Bo would be back soon.

'I haven't seen him. Not since that day the police came round. And he wasn't in earlier when I knocked. Have you seen him at all?'

Betsy shook her head slowly and then looked up, her eyes glinting. 'Shall we go round? Shall we go to see him?'

'We'd have to be quick. I told my mum I wouldn't leave the house. Would your grandma mind?'

'No, she just ask that we tell her where we going.'

We went round straight away. This time it was as if Bo was waiting for us to arrive. The door was flung open as soon as we finished knocking.

'You're right on time,' he said. 'Just in the tick-tock of it.'

Dog rushed up and butted his head into our hands.

'What's going on, Bo?' I asked.

'I've found another way! Another way back to the place, back home. Come on! Come on! There's no time like this present.'

'We go now?' Betsy asked, her eyes wide.

'This is the present!' Bo leaped around the sitting room, blowing out candles, ducking beneath branches and only just missing them. He put on a coat and a scarf and a hat, and then another hat that didn't quite fit on top of the first. And then he reached down for a bag he'd packed and slung it over his shoulder as well.

'How long you go for, Mr Bo?' Betsy asked.

'Well, for however long I'm there, of course, a horse. For ever and a day. Come on, Dog!'

He strode out into the street, with Dog following close behind him.

Betsy and I looked at one another, and I was suddenly sure that she was thinking exactly the same thing as me. We followed him out.

Bo had stopped in front of the bins and the lamppost.

'Bo,' I said gently. 'We can't go with you. We can't go to the place.'

When he spoke, his voice was quiet. Like the tiny rustle of a breeze or the sound of the smallest of creatures as it scurries past.

'I know,' he said. 'That is how I know. It is time for me to go.'

He sighed loudly, his breath moving through his whole body, lifting him up, puffing out his chest and then releasing his spine so that his feet seemed to dig deeper into the ground.

'It was because of you. You did it, Leelu,' he told me.

'What? What did I do?'

'You gave me the most powerful wonder of them all.'

'I did?'

Bo reached into his pocket, his fingers tightly curled around something. 'You needed the wonders when I left them for you. In our little spot – here.' He touched the gap between the bin and the lamppost. 'They helped you when you most needed them. And then, when I needed help, you left something for me.'

He opened his palm, and there lay the small caramel-coloured stone that I'd found in the street and left for Bo in the matchbox with the letter.

'But it's not from the place,' I said straight away. 'I just found it on the way back from school; it won't have powers.'

'Oh, but it does,' Bo said, and he squeezed the stone hard in his hand and muttered something quietly under his breath.

Just then, the ground began to shake.

'What's happening?' Betsy shrieked.

It continued to tremble.

'The place . . .' Bo said. 'It's right here.' He gestured to the bin and the lamppost just in front of us. 'This is it.'

The bin was surrounded with rubbish, as always. Old boxes, torn and full of clothes, had fallen on their side; pieces of what looked like a bed had been dumped next to them. A broken umbrella protruded from the top of some black rubbish sacks, spokes pointing out angrily like a great bird that was about to stretch its wings and take flight.

Bo touched the bin lid lightly, tenderly almost, as though he was stroking Dog when he was scared by a storm. 'People always leave their rubbish here,' he said. 'They always have. And I suppose they always will. They see this just as a place to dump things they want to be rid of. They see the whole world like that. Not as something to treasure, not as something of wonder. I won't forget; I won't forget when I am back home all that I have learned here. I will never stop looking and finding beauty. In all the small things. When I'm home again.'

'But, Bo,' I said gently. 'Where is it?'

'It's right here, Leelu! Right here!'

The ground rumbled again beneath our feet; Betsy almost lost her balance and I reached out a hand to steady her.

Bo touched the little space where he used to wedge things for me to find.

A breeze stirred around us, clattering some leaves and sending them skittering across the road.

But there was nothing more. The ground grew still, unmoving and solid as it ever was. Betsy and I looked at each other anxiously.

That was when we heard it: the low, heavy sound of dragging metal.

The ground shook again.

'Mr Bo!' Betsy cried out.

The bin had slowly started to move aside and underneath it, where there should have been pavement, was a tunnel sloping downwards.

I could see leaves falling at the bottom of the tunnel.

And a light. A light that seemed to sparkle

and dance and move across the tunnel walls like nothing I had ever seen before.

'Here it is!' Bo cried happily. He turned to me. His eyes were full of tears, but they weren't the sad kind of tears because he was smiling too; smiling so hard that his face looked quite different from the one I had got used to.

'You made it happen, Leelu. You don't need the wonders any more, do you?'

I remembered running from the gang, speaking out in class. Bo was right: I didn't need them any more.

'You made the place open up here because of all the power you have found within yourself. It's the most wonderful wonder I've ever had the pleasure of knowing. It's because of you . . . *you* are helping me.'

I looked again down the tunnel of lights; a soft breeze caressed my face. I thought I saw something flitter, a flash of something, and then disappear. It must have been one of the birds that Bo had told us about; the ones that were hardly ever seen, hiding shyly in the branches of the trees. But I'd just seen one!

'So this is a good bye,' said Bo.

He waved his hand a little formally, but then Betsy rushed towards him and we both fell into his arms, hugging him tightly. Somehow I knew that he wouldn't come back, that this was the last time we would see him, and the thought made me squeeze him tighter still.

'Oh, well, this is a very good bye,' Bo said, and then stood up straight. He looked up at the night sky. There was a full moon. 'Time to fly,' he said.

I could see the crater that Dad had pointed out to me and wondered if, wherever he was, he could see it now.

'I think, though, that before we say a very good bye,' Bo said, 'I have just enough wonders for one last thing.'

He threw his bag down onto the ground, and from inside it gathered together a huge number of things – the same things he'd used when he tried to fly. He held them to him, whispering and drawing them to him as they trembled and twitched and shook.

Betsy and I looked around.

Nothing had changed.

'What did you do, Mr Bo?' Betsy asked.

'You'll find out,' he said. 'Soon enough.'

Then he took a step backwards and gave a wobbly-looking bow, only he stepped back a bit too far and almost fell into the tunnel.

'Oops-a-gravy!' Bo said.

I was laughing and crying, all at the same time.

'Goodbye, Bo,' I managed to say through my tears and gasps.

'Goodbye, Leelu. Goodbye, Betsy,' Bo said.

'Don't forget us!' Betsy demanded.

'I won't forget you, Betsy. I won't forget you, Leelu. And you don't forget either.'

'We'll never forget you, Mr Bo,' Betsy said.

'Not me!' Bo said indignantly. 'Don't forget – never forget, Leelu . . . the power you have inside yourself. You have that with you always. You don't need this any longer, but here's just one more – to remember.' He pressed a walnut into my hand.

I grasped it tightly. 'Goodbye, Bo, and thank you. Thank you for everything.'

'Don't forget Dog,' Bo said, and we bent down and hugged Dog's big grey head, and kissed him and hugged him again.

We watched Bo and Dog disappear into the tunnel. As they strode further and further in, they got smaller and smaller, and then, very slowly, the bin began to close over the tunnel. The lights vanished from sight, and the street looked exactly as it always had, the bin and the lamppost and the piles of rubbish as ordinary as ever.

Just then I heard someone shout my name.

'Lee-lu!' It was like the sound of a bell donging, the way my name was being shouted. 'Lee-lu! Lee-lu!'

I looked up and I saw my dad's dear face. He stretched out his arms towards me and I ran to him. I couldn't believe that he was real, that he was really there, until I felt his arms around me. They encircled me and lifted me off the ground and I felt as though I was flying.

'You're here,' I kept saying. 'You're here, you're here,' but through my tears it sounded like I was saying:

We're home.

We're home.

We're home.

Epilogue

We never saw Bo again.

But sometimes, on the days I least expect it, I see a shape of something between the bin and the lamppost.

The first time it was a pine cone – one that was a different shape and size from the one Bo gave me. I have found feathers there; pressed leaves that I've never seen before; sometimes another piece of moss.

Bo has not forgotten us. Maybe one day in the future we will see him when he comes to leave us something.

Maybe.

The things no longer have any powers for me because, as Bo told me, I don't need them any more. They won't make anything happen. But I keep them anyway.

To remember Bo. To remember a time when I found wonders that gave me powers. To remember a time when I found a power within myself.

I treasure them.

Acknowledgements

Huge, billowing thanks to:

My agent, Clare Wallace, not only for her insightful edits and always being brilliant but for bringing this little book-baby into the world at the same time as her little baby was about to arrive too! Your support has meant the world to me.

My editor, Carmen McCullough, who made this book just so much better than it was. Thank you, Carmen, for being so generous with your ideas and enthusiasm – you're a wonder!

The superb teams at Darley Anderson and Penguin Random House, with special thanks to Mary Darby, Emma Winter, Ruth Knowles, Sophie Nelson, Wendy Shakespeare and Jan Bielecki.

Tokunbo Osunbayo, who I can't thank enough for her generosity in answering question after question and always sending back considerate and thoughtful responses, which helped me no end.

My new writing buddy, Adenike Awosanya, who has been a sunny ray of help at the last minute.

My dear friend Leila Woodfield for her invaluable insight into police procedures and patiently explaining it all to me.

My wonderful Ho-Yen, Davies and Arnold family and my family of friends who support me, tell me to keep going, offer up their spare rooms, couches and air beds to me for school visits and always make me laugh.

Dan for helping me every day to be a maker of things.

And finally the wonderful readers and writers who I meet in schools all over the country – you always inspire me to write and to keep writing. Thank *you*.

A note on *The London Eye Mystery* by Siobhan Dowd
Leelu reads a line from *The London Eye Mystery* by the brilliant Siobhan Dowd (on pages 68–69) when she is in the book corner on her first day at school. It's one of my favourite children's books!

**Read on for
exclusive essays by Polly
about why she wrote
*Fly Me Home.***

A Walk in the Woods

I have always loved being close to trees. I grew up very close to a patch of woodland – in fact, I was very lucky to go to a primary school that was right next to the woods – and I return to them at any point that I can.

When I was back visiting home as a grown-up one Christmas, I went for a walk in the woods with my husband, Dan, and my mother-in-law, Sue. The days had been dark and hole-like as they always are during that part of winter, but for those few hours of our walk the light was wonderfully clear. I'd never seen the woods look so beautiful.

After being away from them for a while, they felt like a sort of magical wonderland. Glass drops of water hung from skeletal black branches. Indeed, everything felt like it was glistening and suspended, as though it had all been waiting for us to discover it.

We picked up pine cones and pointed out to each other the lichen upon the knotted patterns of tree bark. We wandered from tree to tree, only stopping to bask in the rays of sunlight that managed to find us through the tangle of branches above.

It was during that walk that I began thinking about a story of a girl who'd never known woodland like this. She'd come on a long journey, perhaps, and had to leave part of herself behind. This tiny gossamer part of an idea made me remember the times I had taken my Year One class to the woods.

At the beginning of autumn term every year, we would take our year group to a tiny wood in south-east London called Sydenham Hill Woods. A lot of them had not been before and many had come over from different countries that had completely different kinds of landscape. My pupils would be in awe of the place, by the shape of an oak leaf, by the feeling of moss.

I remember vividly two children running over frantically to me on one of our trips. 'We've found something!' they told me. 'We've found something!' They dragged me over to a patch of leaves and then both, heads down, studied the ground desperately. It had disappeared. They scratched their heads but carried on looking. 'It was just here,' they told me. 'Right here.' I waited for a while and was almost about to walk away when they started shouting and pointing desperately.

It was a red and white toadstool.

For them, it was pure magic.

'I don't feel I belong anywhere'

My dad was born in Guyana in South America. He moved to London, along with my grandparents and my uncle, aged eleven.

I grew up hearing my dad tell the story of him arriving, and hating, a cold grey London and very much missing the colour, warmth and vibrancy of Guyana. Last year, for the first time, we travelled back to Guyana together. I saw the street where he grew up, walked along the sea wall that made up his journey home from school, tasted the foods that he loved as a child.

I could very much understand, finally, what my dad meant when he would tell me how, after growing up in Guyana, he found London such a cold and unforgiving place when he first arrived.

My grandparents and my uncle travelled out from Guyana before my dad, because my dad had to stay behind to take an exam. (He was going to join them after a few months and lived with his

aunt, uncle and cousin in Georgetown until then.)
The idea of a family splitting and reuniting, which
is a central part of *Fly Me Home,* sparked from this.

Fast forward to my dad growing up, marrying
my mother, fathering my sister and I, and us
growing up in the UK and feeling very much 'at
home' here, and I arrive at the period when I was
teaching my Year One class in Camberwell.

I was faced, for the first time in my life, with a
large number of children who were going through
the very same experience that my father had when
he was a child. They had emigrated to London
and were missing their warmer, more colourful
home countries but nonetheless were forging a
new home in London. Most of them came from
Nigeria or Eritrea.

I very much wanted to capture these children
in the story of Leelu. In my mind, her family is
from Nigeria, although I purposely have not
named the country in order for the reader to bring
their own experience to this.

The idea of what it means to have a 'home
country' and also what 'home' means on its most
basic level to people has been circling in my mind
for years. My father said to me during our trip to
Guyana that he didn't feel he belonged anywhere –
he felt like an outsider now to Guyana because he

had left there, but also an outsider in the UK because he had arrived there, being different. It made me feel unaccountably sad that he felt like this.

I told him that he did belong – he belonged with us, in our family, the place that we created.